A TERRIFYING NEW WEAKNESS . . .

Max took a deep breath and focused on making the connection he would need to heal the gash. Instead of the rush of images from Liz that he expected, he got the same one again and again—the image of him with his eyes rolled back in his head.

Why wasn't it working? Why wasn't he in? Max took another breath. Think of Liz, he told himself. But he only got the same sickening image.

Liz eased his hand away from hers. "It's okay. It's no big deal. Do you have a handkerchief or something? We can just make a bandage."

Max ripped the bottom off his T-shirt and carefully wrapped it across her palm. "Will you be okay to drive?" he asked.

"Yeah." She slid back behind the wheel and pulled back onto the highway. The desert around them felt much darker and dangerous now, now that he knew he no longer had his powers.

ROSWELL HIGH

Available from SIMON PULSE

ROSWELL™

Based on the hit TV series

Available from POCKET BOOKS

ROSWELL
HIGH

THE WATCHER

by

MELINDA METZ

SIMON PULSE
New York   London   Toronto   Sydney   Singapore

This book is a work of fiction. Although the physical setting of the book is Roswell, New Mexico, the high school and its students, names, characters, places, and incidents are either products of the author's imagination or are used fictitiously. Any resemblance to actual events or locales or persons, living or dead, is entirely coincidental.

First SIMON PULSE edition January 2002

Copyright © 1999 by POCKET BOOKS, a division of Simon & Schuster, Inc.
Cover art ™ and © 2000 by Twentieth century Fox Film Corporation.
All rights reserved.

SIMON PULSE
An imprint of Simon & Schuster
Children's Publishing Division
1230 Avenue of the Americas
New York, NY 10020

 Produced by 17th Street Productions, Inc.,
33 West 17th Street, New York, NY 10011

All rights reserved, including the right to reproduce
this book or portions thereof in any form whatsoever.

Printed in U.S.A.
    6 8 10 9 7 5

ISBN: 0-671-77463-8

Max Evans gazed in the bathroom mirror. "Not looking good, chief," he said to his reflection. Hollow cheeks. Bags—more like a full set of luggage—under his eyes. His skin had a transparent, grayish quality. He noticed a zit on his neck. It was actually kind of . . . comforting. It made him feel young.

Max stepped onto the scale. Three pounds less than yesterday. A wave of panic rushed through him. He lost his balance, fell off the scale, and managed to land on the toilet. He covered his face with his hands. Am I having a midlife crisis at sixteen? he wondered. Why do I feel so weak?

He heard a shrill giggle from downstairs. God—I've got to get to work, he thought.

"Uh, I'm leaving now," Max called. He cleared his throat and descended the stairs. "To leave, I have to walk through the living room. I am now moving toward the living room."

Max stepped through the doorway. Oh, man. His sister, Isabel, and her boyfriend, Alex Manes, hadn't taken the hint. They were still all over each other. Max tried not to look as he rushed past them, but he still saw more than he wanted to. Lip lockage.

Some buttons unbuttoned. Hands everywhere.

It just wasn't something a guy needed to see his sister doing. His *little* sister. Okay, she was a junior in high school. But still.

Max slammed out the front door and trotted over to his Jeep, relieved to be out of the house. He swung himself into the driver's seat, turned on the ignition, and backed out the driveway.

He made a left, heading toward the center of Roswell, then cranked the radio and put on his shades against the late afternoon sun. The cool air slid past him, blowing his blond hair off his forehead. He started feeling like a guy in a Jeep ad. An I'm-the-king-of-the-world-up-here-in-my-Jeep feeling.

It had been a while since he'd felt this good. But things were basically going his way. Isabel was with a guy Max actually liked, a guy who treated her right. Yeah, Max wished they would find a slightly more private place for their make-out marathons, but he approved of the whole Isabel-Alex thing.

He smiled. Isabel would be furious if she knew what he was thinking right now. She'd say just because he was her brother that didn't mean he had to give the guys she went out with the seal of approval, like they were sides of beef he thought were fit to be hamburger. She'd say it was none of his business.

But it was. Everyone in the group was his business. He was connected to all six of them. And they were connected to him. Sometimes when they were all hanging out, their auras would swirl together

2

and create one huge aura filled with colors. Even when they were apart, that feeling of oneness lingered within him. Max didn't think he could feel this good if something was really wrong with one of the others.

Isabel and Alex were certainly happy. Maybe even a little too happy for Max's taste. He was almost scared to think of them getting any happier—they might break a natural law or something. That took care of two of the six.

Maria DeLuca was doing okay, too, especially considering that she'd almost died on them last week. She'd found a ring that contained one of the Stones of Midnight. It gave her psychic powers—by merely thinking of someone, she could experience their thoughts and emotions. Unfortunately bounty hunters from Max's home planet were tracking the stolen Stone. They tried to kill Maria, and they probably would have.

But Michael Guerin, Max's best friend, faced the bounty hunters with her and basically saved her. Now the worst thing Michael had to deal with was adjusting to his latest foster home. His new foster parents, the Pascals, had a lot of rules, but they seemed to really care about the kids who lived with them. That had to count for something.

And Liz . . . Admit it, Max thought. Now you've come to the real reason you're feeling good. Liz Ortecho doesn't hate you anymore.

He had come so close to permanently messing things up with Liz. He'd kissed her and then told her he wanted to be just friends. Then he'd kissed her *again* and told her he wanted to be just friends *again*. And then when she decided to go out with another guy, Max had followed her like some kind of lunatic stalker. Not exactly something a *friend* would do.

So Liz had gone into Max-hating mode. But when Maria got hurt, it took all six of them to get her through—so they put Max's maddening fickleness aside for the time being. They'd managed to find a way back to being friends. Just friends. But friends.

A new song came on the radio. One of those whiny, wailing chick songs about the pain of love. Not what Max wanted to hear right now. Not when he was actually feeling decent for once. He did a fast button punch to change the station.

A drum solo pounded out. It was loud. Way too loud. Louder than it would be if he were sitting next to one of those huge amps at a concert. Max fumbled for the volume control and turned the knob to the left. But the drums got louder. He felt as if the drumsticks were slamming into his brain. Stabbing through the gray matter.

Max pulled over to the curb and stopped the car. He snapped the radio off. The drumming stopped. But there were still so many sounds. A car honked as it passed him. Max jerked his head back and gritted his teeth. The honk seemed to pierce his delicate eardrum like a needle.

Max shoved his hands against his ears. He tried

to keep from screaming. The sound of his own howl of pain would be agony.

He squeezed his eyes shut, leaned down, and pressed his forehead against the steering wheel. His hands weren't blocking out enough of the noise. He could still hear car wheels against the street, a bird chirping in one of the trees, two girls giggling. He could hear electricity pulsing through the power lines over his head. And the leaves of the trees brushing together. And his own blood rushing through his veins. It was too much. He couldn't take it.

Then it stopped. As if some giant hand had reached down and lowered the cosmic volume control. Max could hear only dim, muffled sounds through his hands. He slowly opened his eyes. He watched a car drive by. He could hardly hear it.

Max moved his hands a few inches away from his ears. He held them poised there, ready to slap them back in place if he needed to. But the sounds were . . . just normal sounds. Some louder than others, but none getting even close to the pain-inducing level.

What *was* that? Max thought. He glanced around the street. He spotted a woman a few houses down, working in her garden. She seemed too absorbed in her work to have experienced anything like what Max had.

Of course she hadn't. Maybe there had been a screwup at the radio station, something that made it blast out music at eardrum-popping levels. But that couldn't explain the volume on cars and birds and power lines. No, whatever that was had happened *inside* him.

Max let out a long, shuddering breath and lowered his hands to the wheel. He waited a few more minutes to make sure he wasn't going to get hit with another sound blast, then he pulled away from the curb.

He felt the tension in his neck and shoulders and arms as he drove. Even his fingers were curled too tightly around the wheel. Relax, he told himself. Just take a deep breath and relax. His body wouldn't obey—it was bracing itself for the next assault.

But it didn't come. Max made it to the UFO museum without even a flash of the mega–sound blast. He maneuvered the Jeep into an empty spot in the parking lot. Should I ask Ray about what happened? he wondered. Maybe it was an alien thing.

But Ray Iburg didn't like being asked questions about alien things. He said that even though Max, Isabel, and Michael were from his home planet, earth was their home now. He didn't want them to spend their lives thinking about some other place.

Even though Max suspected that Ray spent a lot of time thinking about home—*his* home.

When Max first found out that Ray was an alien, too, he'd gotten this picture in his mind. He'd never admitted it to anyone else, but he'd thought he and Ray would get a Luke Skywalker–Yoda kind of thing going, where Ray would impart all his wisdom to Max, tell Max about his parents, teach him how to refine his powers, that kind of stuff. Okay, maybe it was dorky. But that's what he'd thought.

It hadn't turned out like that. Ray had told him and Michael about their parents' death. He'd shown them a hologram re-creation of the spaceship crashing in the desert outside Roswell back in 1947. And he'd told them how he brought their incubation pods from the ship to the desert cave where they would be safe during the years it took them to develop to maturity. He'd even shown them a few new things that they could do with their powers, things that might help protect them against being discovered by Sheriff Valenti. Plus he'd completely been there for them when a group of alien bounty hunters came after Maria.

That was all. Ray was happy for Max to keep working at the museum. But he acted as if he and Max were just two ordinary humans. And he wanted Max to act the same way.

Max wanted so much more from Ray. He wanted Ray to teach him the history of their planet—its culture and all its phenomena. Ray might tell him if the intense volume thing Max had just experienced was alien related. But then he'd probably clam up.

Max climbed out of the Jeep and crossed the parking lot. He took off his sunglasses and hooked them over the edge of his T-shirt.

"I found a great painting of foo fighters," Ray announced the second Max walked through the door. "Come check it out." He started toward the back of the museum without waiting for a reply.

"I didn't know Foo Fighters had any UFO connection," Max commented as he followed Ray.

"Don't say that so loud," Ray cautioned. He took a quick glance around for tourists, but the museum's few customers were flipping through the T-shirt rack on the other side of the place. "People pay good money to come in here and enjoy their wacky human theories. Myself, I think it's the World War Two version of an urban legend. That generation's hook-handed man in the back of a car."

"Whoa. I'm talking about the rock band here, Ray. And you would be talking about?"

Ray turned the corner and nodded at a massive oil painting of an old fighter plane being chased by what looked like balls of orange and green fire. "The band got their name from these foo fighters. That's what people called the incredibly fast, glowing balls and silver disks reported to follow planes and ships in the European and Pacific theaters during the war. The UFologist types think they were UFOs," Ray explained. He pointed at Max. "And if anyone asks you about them, you believe the same thing. Got it?"

"I live to deceive the public," Max said. Now seemed like a good time to ask about what had happened in the car.

Ray tilted his head to one side. "I think that painting is crooked. Good thing I left the ladder out."

"I'll fix it." Max hurried over and climbed up to the second-highest step. He pushed the corner of the painting down about half an inch. "How does that look?" he asked.

He stood way too close to it to tell. The painting was so big, it filled most of his field of vision. Max stared at it, transfixed. The orange and green balls practically vibrated with color. He felt as if they were flying toward him. They were so bright, they almost seemed to glow.

"Ray? Is it straight?" Max repeated. He felt his mouth moving, forming the words. But no sound came out. He realized the museum had become absolutely silent.

"Ray!" he shouted. He could feel the muscles in his throat working. But he couldn't force out a sound.

He started to turn and look for Ray, but his gaze locked on the colors of the painting. They were brighter now. So bright, they made his eyes burn.

Look away! Now! he ordered himself. But the colors were so beautiful. So vivid. Mesmerizing. The green and orange filled his vision. It was like staring directly into the sun. And he couldn't force his gaze away.

His eyes felt like hot coals jammed into his head. The green and orange balls exploded in front of him. Filling his vision with searing bits of color.

Then a wave of dizziness swept through Max, and the world went black. He couldn't feel the ladder under his feet. And he was falling.

He knew he was only a few feet off the ground. He should have landed instantaneously. But he kept hurtling through the dark, silent void. Spinning, twisting, rolling. But always falling.

Then it was over. He could feel the museum's tile floor under his back. He could hear Ray's voice saying his name.

He opened his eyes a crack. He saw blobs of color, but none had the effect of the painting's green and orange balls of fire. He opened his eyes the rest of the way and sat up.

"Are you okay? What happened?" Ray asked.

Max scrubbed his face with his fingers. "I was hoping you would tell me," he muttered.

Ray turned to the group of tourists who had gathered. "He's fine. You can all go back to what you were doing. Don't miss the crop circle exhibit," he told them. Then he helped Max to his feet. "Come on, I'll get you something to drink."

Ray led Max to a table at the back of the museum's little coffee shop. "You want water, a Lime Warp, what?"

Max shook his head. All he wanted was information. And fast. "Nothing. I just need you to help me figure out what's going on. I was standing on the ladder, and everything was normal. Then the green and orange in the painting got brighter and brighter until they were burning my eyes. Then it's like I went blind. And deaf—that actually happened first. And then I was falling. It was like I'd fallen off a skyscraper or something. It took me forever to hit the ground."

Saying all that out loud . . . it made him feel like

10

a loon. Maybe he had a fever or something.

Ray sat down across from Max and studied his face intensely. "Is this the first time anything like this has happened?" he asked.

"On the way here something weird happened, too. All the sounds got incredibly loud. I thought my eardrums were going to explode. And then it just stopped. Everything sounded normal again," Max told him. He lowered his voice. "I thought at first maybe it was an *alien* thing. But maybe it's—"

"You thought right," Ray jumped in. "Have you had any spells of extreme fatigue?"

"Uh, I guess, sort of. Once or twice," Max admitted, thinking back over the past few weeks. He hadn't really thought anything about those spells.

Ray nodded, his expression grave. "You've just described the first stage of the *akino.*"

"And that would be?" Max asked. He struggled to stay calm and rational, even though there was something in Ray's tone that made Max's anxiety level spike. Not to mention the streaks of sickly yellow invading the blue-and-green whorls of Ray's aura.

"Our race has a . . . collective consciousness," Ray explained. "It's like a psychic Internet. All the knowledge, all the life experience, all the emotions of all of our people are there in the consciousness. When a young person reaches maturity, he or she is able to make the connection to the consciousness for the first time. This rite of passage is called the *akino.* The physical symptoms you've experienced—the bursts of heightened sensation, the fatigue—are signals that it is time for you to make your connection."

Max breathed a sigh of relief. "So, it's a good thing, right?" Actually it sounded more than good. It sounded awesome. The collective consciousness would hold the answer to every question Max had about his home planet, his people.

He felt some of the tightness in his muscles ease a little. He didn't have some hideous aliens-only disease. And Ray knew exactly what was going on. He could walk Max through the whole *akino* deal.

"Usually it would be a cause for celebration," Ray agreed. "Like a human bar mitzvah or a wedding. But—"

"I know, I know. I live on earth. This is my home. I shouldn't waste time thinking about a place I'll never go," Max interrupted.

"That's not what I was going to say," Ray told him. "There is no question that you must join the collective consciousness. And soon. But we're too far away. You need . . . you need the communication crystals. And they're on the ship."

"The ship? The ship disappeared after the crash, remember? We don't know where it is," Max protested. "Michael and I have been looking for it practically our whole lives."

Ray reached across the table and grabbed Max's hand. Which was weird. Ray wasn't one of those touchy-feely guys. Max felt his muscles retighten until his entire body ached.

"Max, if you don't connect to the consciousness, you will die," Ray said slowly and clearly.

Die. The word sucked all the air out of Max's lungs and left him gasping.

No. It couldn't be. A few dizzy spells could not possibly equal a fatal disease.

"Wait," he protested. "I've lived on earth my whole life. You have no way of knowing how that's changed my body. You can't be sure I'll respond the same way I would have if I was on our home planet," Max said in a rush. He tried to pull his hand free, but Ray tightened his grip.

"You're right. I don't know how growing to maturity on this planet has affected you. But here's what I do know," Ray answered. "I know that the experiences you described to me—the painfully loud sounds and bright colors—they're almost exactly what I went through myself when it was my *akino* time."

"That doesn't mean crap. I thought you were supposed to be a scientist or something. Don't you think you're making a huge assumption here?" Max demanded. He gave his hand another wrench, and this time Ray let it go.

Max crossed his arms, tucking his hand against his body. But he could still feel the tremors running through it.

"Maybe you're right," Ray said gently. He used his sleeve to rub a coffee stain off one of the little alien faces decorating the table. "But just in case you're not, I—"

Max felt like he was about to lose it. He could already feel a lump growing in his throat, and his eyes were getting so wet that another blink might bring tears.

He sprang out of his chair so quickly that it toppled. He caught it before it hit the ground and slammed it back in place. Then he took a long breath, pulling it deep into his lungs. "What do you want me to do today?" he asked. "I know you're not paying me to grow my hair."

Ray gave a small smile—whether because Max had used one of Ray's favorite expressions or because of his amazingly obvious subject change, Max wasn't sure. "Why don't you go into the storage area and see if you can find any more foo fighter stuff for the display?"

"On it." Max took three steps away from the table, then turned. "Ray, if you're right and I do have to connect to the consciousness, how much time do I have?"

"It's hard to say exactly," Ray admitted. "Maybe months. Maybe days."

"Is it closing time?" Maria DeLuca whined. "Please let it be closing time." She slid her left heel out of her new shoe and studied the massive blister growing there.

"Five minutes," her best friend, Liz Ortecho, told her. "I don't know why you wore those shoes to work, anyway."

"In these shoes I actually approach tallness," Maria explained. "You just don't know what it's like when you're my height. People act like I'm some kind of mutant—part girl, part puppy. Strangers pat me on the head."

That was the truth. Kind of. Maria *did* like being taller. But if she was totally and completely honest, she chose the shoes more because of what they did for her legs than what they did for her height. She'd have to live in the gym to get the killer calves those shoes gave her.

Liz's dad had broken down and bought new uniforms for the wait staff at the Crashdown Café. They were basically *Men in Black* rip-offs. Except Maria had gone for the black skirt instead of the black pants. And in her new skirt, with the new shoes, well, it's not like she was suddenly as beautiful as Liz or anything. But the combo definitely got her a few more looks, and a few more tips, than usual.

Unfortunately the guy she most wanted to do the looking, Michael Guerin, hadn't shown up today. He hung out at the café a lot. Of course, he never bothered to tell her in advance when he was going to stop by. That would make things way too easy on her. And her feet.

"People don't pat you on the head because you're short," Liz explained. "It's because your hair looks so springy. People want to touch it to see if it will go *boing.*"

"Oh, thanks for clarifying that." Maria tried to shoot Liz an annoyed look but ruined it by breaking into giggles.

"I'll collect the sugar bowls, and you can start filling them," Liz said. "That way you can stay behind the counter . . . where probably no one will notice that you aren't wearing shoes."

Maria immediately kicked off the torture devices masquerading as footwear. Aaaah! She gave her toes a happy wiggle, then knelt down to grab the sugar. As she reached for the box, the opening notes of the *Close Encounters* theme rang out.

The door chime. Someone was coming in. Was it Michael? Without standing up, Maria grabbed her left shoe and jammed her foot in. She felt an explosion of wetness on her heel as her blister burst. She ignored the pain and shoved on the right shoe, gripping the counter for balance. Then she slowly stood up, trying for a casual, I-have-no-idea-the-door-chime-even-rang coolness.

Her casual smile faded when she saw Elsevan DuPris standing in front of the cash register. The guy gave her the creeps. It's not that he wasn't friendly. In fact, he was a little too friendly. And his southern accent, it was a little too southern. It just sounded fake. Which brought up the question— why? Why would a person stroll around dressed in a white suit and white shoes, twirling a walking stick and talking in an obviously fake southern accent?

DuPris was the editor-owner of the *Astral Projector,* Roswell's all-alien tabloid. So you had to expect the guy to be a *little* eccentric. But he was even eccentric in his eccentricity.

"I'm doing a poll for my little paper, and I wondered if you'd be good enough to assist me," DuPris drawled. "I believe there is a connection between a person's ability to roll their tongue and alien inbreeding somewhere in their lineage. I thought it would be interesting to see if we have a greater number of people with this attribute in our fair town, for obvious reasons."

Liz rushed up to the counter and dropped a load of the flying-saucer-shaped sugar bowls. "Sounds interesting. I'd love to see your data sometime, but we're closed now, so—"

"So I'll say good night to you young ladies. And I'll be sure to bring these, uh, experimental results

17

by," DuPris said. He tipped his white Panama hat and sauntered out the door. Liz followed him and locked it the second he stepped outside.

Maria smiled as she kicked off her shoes for the second time. Liz definitely knew how to put people in their place when they needed it. If she hadn't been around, Maria probably would have done the tongue-rolling thing for DuPris, feeling like an idiot the whole time. Then she'd probably have been sucked into a long conversation with him, making feeble comments about needing to get back to work but not actually being able to escape.

Liz returned with an armful of ketchup bottles and lowered them to the counter. Maria rolled her tongue at her.

"So you're part alien," Liz teased. "Anything else you've been hiding?"

"You already know I'm really a man, so I guess not," Maria answered. She picked up the sugar box and started refilling the bowls.

"Just checking," Liz said. "Keeping secrets from me is a serious violation. I don't want to have to bring you up in front of the best friend review board." She ducked behind the counter and headed into the kitchen.

Maria shot a glance after her. Liz was doing that kind of joking around that has a little truth lurking somewhere in the background. And the truth was that Maria hadn't been totally up front with her best friend lately.

Liz returned to the counter with a big plastic jug

of ketchup and a funnel. "Okay, okay. I wore these shoes because I was hoping Michael would come by," Maria blurted. "And yes, I have a totally hopeless, pathetic thing for him."

Liz laughed. "I knew that already. I was actually talking about the whole psychic powers episode. How could you not tell me about something so big?" She unscrewed the top on the closest ketchup bottle and stuck in the funnel.

Maria felt a blush creeping up her neck. In a second her whole face would be red. "I still feel like such a loser. I can't believe I actually thought I was psychic. You should have seen me. I was so jazzed, thinking I had this amazing gift. It was so incredible to hold something that belonged to a person and then be able to *see* exactly what they were doing. And healing Sassy. That was awesome."

"You shouldn't feel like a loser. How could you have known?" Liz asked. "Like you were supposed to think, 'Hey, maybe that ring I found at the mall has an alien power stone in it.'"

Liz pushed the ketchup bottle away and turned to face Maria. "What I want to know is why you didn't tell me what was going on," she said, her dark brown eyes serious and watchful.

I really hurt her feelings, Maria realized. Duh. Like I wouldn't have been hurt if I found out Liz had been keeping some big secret from me.

"I wasn't trying to shut you out or anything," Maria explained. "It's just that you weren't doing too well. You were so messed up over the Max sitch.

19

There didn't seem to be a good time to bring it up."

"Maria, no matter what's going on with me, I still want to know what's going on with you," Liz said. "If you'd told me, maybe I could have—"

"Stop," Maria interrupted. "You and Max act like you're responsible for everybody else's problems. It's so not true."

She gave a long sigh. "You know what, if I told you, there is a chance you would have stopped me before . . ."

"Before you almost died," Liz filled in.

"Yeah. And that's probably why I didn't say anything to you. I didn't want to be stopped. I told myself I wasn't clueing you in to what was going on because you were devastated by the whole Max thing. But that's only partly true. I basically knew I was playing with something dangerous. I kept getting blackouts, even a nasty nosebleed."

Maria heard Liz give a sharp intake of breath, but she didn't stop talking. She had to get this out. "But I didn't want to stop using the powers—or be stopped by you—until I found out where Michael's parents' ship was being kept."

"So this was all about Michael," Liz said.

"I had some stupid idea that if I could do that for him . . ." Maria shook her head hard. "Forget it. It's too stupid to even say."

"It's not stupid," Liz told her. "Well, okay, it's stupid. But understandable stupid. Not just stupid stupid."

"That makes me feel better," Maria mumbled.

Then she met Liz's gaze directly. "It does. It feels good to have told you the total truth."

"So, we're agreed. No more secrets," Liz said.

"No more secrets," Maria promised. She pushed up the hinged section of the counter and stepped through, then grabbed a couple of the sugar bowls and headed toward the closest row of tables.

"Maria," Liz called.

Maria turned to face her. She should have known Liz wouldn't let her off the hook without more of a lecture on putting her life in jeopardy.

"Why don't you tell Michael how you feel?" Liz asked.

"Why?" Maria repeated. She blushed, then hugged the sugar bowls more tightly to her chest. "Because if I do that, he might laugh. Or he might start acting all weird around me. Or he might just avoid me." Maria could hear her voice shaking with emotion, but she kept going. "He might stop climbing through my window late at night . . . and I don't think I could stand that."

"You know what else might happen?" Liz asked gently. "He might tell you he feels the same way about you."

"All right, so I'm thinking, for this week's list, 'Bills That I'd Rather Be Than Me.' Number one: Bill Gates. Number two: Billy Baldwin. Number three: Mr. Bill. What do you guys think? Is that stupid?"

Same spot in the quad as at lunch yesterday. Same people. Practically the same conversation, with Alex going on about ideas for the lists he put on his web site, Liz thought. Then she smiled. She wouldn't want it any other way.

"How about terms for guys who spend way too much time thinking about their web page?" Michael suggested. "Number one—wedgie boy."

"Hey, you know how many hits I get? My lists have a following. It's practically a cult thing," Alex protested.

"Number two—big goober," Maria suggested.

Liz noticed that Isabel wasn't jumping in to defend her man. She wasn't sure what she thought about the Alex-Isabel hookup. It's not that she didn't like Isabel. Liz was actually feeling closer to her all the time. But she and Alex . . . they just weren't an obvious couple. They had some of that

23

I'm-a-little-bit-country/I'm-a-little-bit-rock-and-roll deal going on.

Isabel was the ultimate It girl. The girl who got noticed and envied, lusted after, hated, or some combination thereof by pretty much everyone.

Alex was, well—

"Or how about geek child," Maria volunteered, snickering.

No, Alex wasn't exactly geeky. But he didn't stand out of the crowd the way Isabel did. You had to get to know him before you realized how totally cool he was. He had this great, wacked sense of humor, and when he believed in something, he absolutely would not back down. Plus he had amazing green eyes, rich reddish brown hair, and a lean, muscular body.

It wasn't hard for Liz to see why a girl would want to be with him. Lots of girls, actually. But Isabel? Liz shook her head. Hey, if it worked, it worked. And it seemed to be working.

"Come on, Liz, Max. Join the fun. Take your best shot," Alex told her. He slammed his fists into his chest. "I can take it."

"Uh, cyberweenie?" Liz offered.

"Does anyone want the rest of this sandwich?" Max asked.

"I'll take it," Alex and Michael said together.

Liz shot a sharp look at Max. He'd pretty much fainted last week, out of the blue. Since then she'd asked him a few times if he was feeling okay, and he kept insisting that he was. But she believed in going by the facts—the fact that he seemed lethargic a lot of the time, the fact that he wasn't eating much, the fact that his skin had a slightly grayish tone. And the facts made her doubt him.

She didn't want a repeat of the Maria situation. If there was something wrong with Max, she needed to know about it.

The bell rang. Isabel and Maria slowly headed to their English class. Michael and Alex took off in opposite directions. Leaving her alone with Max.

"Ready for another adventure in the wonderful world of science?" he asked her as he shoved himself to his feet.

He sounded normal. Except that his voice was a little too bright, like he was straining for his usual tone and overshooting it.

"Always," Liz answered. She heard that same quality in her voice, that see-there's-really-nothing-wrong sound.

This was so ridiculous. She loved Max, and she knew he loved her. Yeah, they had agreed—well, Max had insisted, and Liz had agreed—that they would be just friends.

But did that mean they had to be so phony? Why couldn't he trust her with the truth—whatever it was? Why couldn't she just tell him to cut the bull and tell her what was going on?

Maybe it's because we're still being careful with each other, Liz thought as they made their way to the main building. We've managed to create this friend facade over the mess of our relationship. But it's not that strong. Maybe we both know it would be very easy to destroy it.

Liz led the way inside and over to the staircase. She and Max climbed in silence. She could hear his breathing pick up as they got near the top. Another fact to add to the pile. Max was in good shape. A few stairs shouldn't get him breathing hard.

Liz shortened her stride as they walked down the hall to give Max a chance to catch his breath. "I read over the experiment we're doing today. It sounds pretty interesting," she said as they entered the classroom and took their places in their usual lab station.

Max didn't answer.

Liz Ortecho, Queen of Idle Chitchat, she thought.

"We have another long one today," Ms. Hardy announced. "You can go ahead and get started. I'll work my way to all of you, but flag me down if you have questions."

"I'll set up the Bunsen burner," Max said.

"I'll weigh the samples," Liz volunteered.

At least this was something they didn't have to fake. They both took their lab work seriously. And they were a good team.

Liz pulled the scale out of the cupboard—pretty grimy. She stepped up to the sink, turned on the water, dampened a long piece of brown paper towel, and scrubbed the scale clean. *Don't these amateur scientists know that a dirty scale can corrupt all your data?* she thought.

"Max," Ms. Hardy called from a lab station near the front of the room, "that flame is much too high."

Liz glanced over. Ms. Hardy was right. The Bunsen burner's flame was inches above where it needed to be. And the tip of Max's finger was right in the middle of the fire!

The odor of cooking meat hit her nose, and her throat clenched in a dry gag. What was he doing? Couldn't he feel that he was burning himself? Liz shot out her hand and twisted off the gas. The flame disappeared.

"Max, are you okay?" Liz demanded. "Let me see your finger." She reached for his hand.

"It's fine," Max snapped. He jerked his hand away.

"It can't be fine," she shot back. "You were holding it *in* the fire. And your skin . . . Max, your skin was *bubbling.*"

"I've got to go change for practice," Isabel said, but she didn't pull away from Alex. What he was doing just felt too good. Except that the way he was leaning into her was jamming her lower back against one of the bleacher's metal steps.

"I could help you," Alex mumbled against her ear, his warm breath sending spikes of pleasure through her body. He reached between them and started unbuttoning her blouse.

27

Isabel grabbed his hand. "Thanks, but I think I can handle it." Their position back alongside the bleachers would prevent most people from seeing them. But still.

Alex slowly rebuttoned the buttons. Then he smoothed down her collar and brushed a lock of her hair back in place. Sometimes he could be so tender. It made Isabel feel like she was turning all liquid inside.

"Is-a-bel!" Stacey Scheinin's high, baby-doll voice echoed through the gym. "Get a move on. You can't afford to miss one minute of practice. We're going to watch a video of our last halftime show before we start. You'll see what I mean."

"Want me to kill her for you?" Alex asked.

"Maybe for my birthday," Isabel answered. She gave him a quick gotta-go kiss and jumped away before he could get his hands on her again.

"Remember tonight's the night you're having dinner at my house," Alex said.

"Like I'd forget," Isabel answered. How could she? She'd been trying to think of a good excuse to get out of it all week. She'd met his mom once for about two seconds, and she seemed nice enough. But his dad sounded obnoxious. And then there were two of his brothers. Alex hardly ever talked about them, so she didn't really know what to expect.

"I'll see you in a few hours." She turned around and headed to the locker room. She was careful not to hurry. Stacey was holding the door for her, giving her a little frown that was meant to be intimidating. Isabel flashed a quick smile to show that it wasn't.

"Everyone, Isabel needs our help," Stacey called as she followed Isabel down the row of lockers. "She has a new boy who is in serious need of a makeover. I know you've all seen him. Any suggestions? I was thinking maybe an 'I heart Isabel' tattoo."

Isabel thought about saying she'd just been doing a little charity work, giving Alex a thrill. It's not like he could hear her or anything. He'd never know.

But she'd feel like scum. It wasn't worth it.

"Yeah, a tattoo's a great idea. Isabel could get a matching one," someone called from the next row.

One of Stacey's court. They all copied that affected little voice of hers. Pathetic sheep.

"He doesn't look like he has a lot of money, going by his clothes, anyway," another Staceyette commented. "I say he should go with something cheap. Like a nice paper bag over the head."

Yeah, and if Stacey was going out with him, you'd be saying how gorgeous he was, Isabel thought. She sat down on the wooden bench in front of her locker and twisted in the combination. It wouldn't open. She tried it again. Still wouldn't open. Then she realized that her locker was the next one over.

"What else?" Stacey called, bouncing on her toes. "One tattoo and one paper bag's not going to do it. Come on, our teammate needs our help."

Tish Okabe sat down next to Isabel. "I think Alex is a cutie," she said loudly.

"You think everyone is a cutie," at least three girls yelled back.

Isabel snapped open her lock, pulled it off, and swung open the metal door. It was nice of Tish to defend Alex. But Isabel knew she should be doing it herself. She just didn't know what to say. Stacey would pounce on anything that came out of her mouth and twist it around. Maybe it was better just to ignore her.

Yeah, Isabel thought. You keep telling yourself that. Or you could just grow a backbone, as Alex would say.

"I'm not surprised you can't figure out what I see in Alex, Stacey," Isabel said coolly. "It's like how some people would rather eat a burger than filet mignon. Their palates just aren't sophisticated enough to appreciate the difference."

"Aw, isn't that sweet? She's standing by her man," Stacey cooed.

Isabel felt like knocking Stacey on her butt.

"You know who I think is filet mignon?" Corrine Williams asked Isabel. "Your brother. I'm having a party on Friday. Tell Max to come. And bring that other guy you're always hanging around with—Michael Guerin."

"Yeah," Stacey jumped in. "If you get both of them there, then I guess you can bring Alex, too."

She licked her finger and made a little one-point-for-me mark in the air.

Chalk one up while you can, Princess of Petty. Because you don't have a snowball's chance at Max or Michael, Isabel thought. But she couldn't help feeling a sting of shame that Alex didn't make the cool-people cut.

"I don't have a big desire to be a squid. Except maybe a squid like Squidly Diddly," Alex told his brother as they set the table. "Or was he an octopus? No. Had to be a squid. Hence the Squidly."

Jesse just stared at him, in a have-you-lost-your-mind kind of way.

"It's a cartoon. It's on the Cartoon Network," Alex explained. "They have *Speed Racer. Scooby Doo.* All the classics."

"First of all, marines aren't called squids—that's the navy. Marines are called jarheads. Not by punks like you, though—you'd just earn yourself a beating if you tried it," Jesse told him. "And second, do they have that one cartoon, *Josie and the Pussycats*? Because those Pussycats are hot."

Alex laughed. Jesse was definitely the coolest of his three brothers. Yeah, he had just given Alex the speech, the "you have got to be a military man" speech. But at least Jesse occasionally thought about, and even talked about, other stuff. Unlike their dad. And their other brother Harry, who was also home for a visit.

Fortunately for Alex his third big brother,

33

Robert, couldn't make it home this time. Alex didn't think he could handle a four-part surround sound lecture on why he should go straight into the military after grad. The three-pronged attack mounted by Jesse, Harry, and his father had been rough enough. And Alex suspected it still wasn't over.

"Being a marine, it changes your life," Jesse said.

Nope. It definitely wasn't over.

"It's like you have a whole new family," Jesse continued. "Or at least like you have a bigger family."

A bigger family. Yeah. That sounded real appealing.

Harry wandered into the dining room and plopped down on one of the chairs. "You girls are doing such a nice job with the table," he cooed.

"Thanks. We put a pretty red bowl on the kitchen floor for you," Jesse shot back. "We thought you might be more comfortable in there since we have company coming and you still haven't quite mastered the use of silverware."

"Company?" Harry asked. "Oh, right. We get to meet Alex's little girlfriend."

Little girlfriend. Alex knew his brother was expecting some geek girl. He couldn't wait to see Harry's face when he got an eyeful of Isabel. Okay, that sounded a little piggish. And he apologized to the goddesses of womanhood or whatever. But it was still going to feel pretty good to show Harry—and Jesse, and even the old man—that little brother was playing in the big leagues.

Harry leaned back until his chair was balanced

on two legs. "So, I just got off the phone with Alice Shaffer," he told Alex.

Alex put the last fork in place. "Who?" he asked.

"Your principal," Harry answered. "She said you never gave her the ROTC application materials." He rocked back and forth, making the chair legs creak. "She said you've never mentioned the ROTC to her period."

Alex felt like kicking that chair right out from under his brother. Just because their dad was totally obsessed with starting an ROTC program at the high school, why did Harry have to get all involved?

"The three of us have an appointment with her tomorrow at four," Harry continued. "Dad wants you to come," he informed Jesse. "He thinks you and I will be great and shining examples of what the ROTC program can do. You better keep your mouth shut so you don't blow it."

"I lost the application Dad gave me," Alex said. "I'm waiting to get a new one in the mail. There's no point in having a meeting without it."

Not a very creative excuse. Only about half a step above the dog ate it, which he couldn't have used because they didn't have a dog.

"Got it covered," Harry answered. "Dad told me to bring one with me."

Oh, happy day.

Jesse shot Alex a semisympathetic look. "You didn't actually think you were getting out of it, did you?"

"I guess not," Alex admitted.

But he'd been doing everything he could to block his dad on this one. He'd thought of it as practice. A way of preparing for the big battle—the one where he told the Major that he wasn't planning on a military career.

Just because you get muscled into helping set up an ROTC program at school, and being unable to escape joining said program, doesn't mean that you'll end up in the military, Alex promised himself.

He wished he believed that.

"We should think about what we're going to say," Harry told Jesse. "Alex's principal didn't sound all that excited about the program."

"I'm not saying anything, remember?" Jesse answered.

"Fine," Harry said. "Alex, I want to go over what clubs and organizations you already have at school. That way I—"

The doorbell rang, interrupting him. "I'll get it." Alex bolted before Harry could say another word. He swung open the door, and a big, doofy grin spread across his face. He didn't think he'd ever been so happy to see Isabel.

"Hey, you look really beautiful," he said, careful to keep his voice low. Harry and Jesse would fall on the floor laughing if they heard him.

But Isabel did look beautiful . . . as usual. Except tonight she looked dressed-up beautiful. She was wearing this shiny, clingy dress with embroidered roses growing up from the bottom. And her blond hair fell down across her shoulders in perfect waves.

"Thanks," Isabel answered. "So, are you going to introduce me?"

Alex turned around and saw his brothers standing there. And his dad halfway down the stairs. His stomach kind of seized up for a minute. His dad tended to have that effect on him.

"That's my brother Jesse. That's Harry. And that's my dad," Alex said.

"And I'm Isabel Evans," she added. She shook hands with all of them.

Duh! He forgot *half* the introduction! But Isabel jumped right in there. She was good at impressing people and making them feel at ease. At least when she felt like bothering.

"Why are you all standing around in the hall?" his mother called. "Come on in the living room."

They all obediently trooped in. Alex and Isabel sat on the love seat. Usually he'd put his arm around her. But it just felt too weird in front of his family.

"So, Isabel . . . Alex is helping me figure out how to get your principal to agree to an ROTC program at your school," Harry told her. "Any ideas?"

What a butt kisser. Alex was sure that Harry just wanted to show his dad that he was on top of the ROTC situation. Harry was twenty-two years old . . . and still living to please daddy.

"Maybe you could try telling her that it's sort of like cheerleading," Isabel answered. "Stacey Scheinin, the head cheerleader, is pretty much a drill sergeant. Except she has this little Minnie Mouse voice."

Alex braced himself for the explosion. He didn't think his dad would like the cheerleader-ROTC comparison. But his dad just laughed. And kept on laughing as Isabel launched into an impersonation of Stacey and the other girls on the squad.

His mom and brothers were laughing, too. And the little glances Harry and Jesse kept shooting at Isabel made it pretty clear they thought she was hot.

But Isabel was *his* girl. Alex enjoyed being the enviable sibling, for once in his short life.

Max picked up the lighter and turned it over and over in his hands. He could see the fluid sloshing around inside through the green plastic.

He flicked it on and stared at the flame, thinking about the Bunsen burner in lab class. That flame had dazzled his eyes until all he could see was a wall of flickering orange and yellow. The whole lab had disappeared. Liz had disappeared. And Max had been surrounded by a beautiful, horrible fire that felt like it was melting his eyes with the brilliance of its colors.

Liz said he'd been holding his finger in the flame, but he hadn't felt anything except the sensation of his eyes dripping out of their sockets and mixing with the flames.

Max put down the lighter and clicked open his laptop. He selected a file called *fertilizer.* He'd called the file that because every once in a while his mom or dad or Isabel borrowed his computer, and he thought the file name *akino* would get their attention. So would the word *death. Fertilizer,* that wasn't something that any of them would be tempted to take a peek at. And it seemed appropriate. Fertilizer, that's what he would become. Something to help the flowers grow. Worm food.

Can you say morbid? Max asked himself.

Max typed in the date and added a short description of what he'd experienced in the lab. When he got enough data, he planned to start charting it. How many bursts of intense vision, how many of intense sound, how many of . . . whatever new symptoms appeared. He wanted to get a sense of how fast the *akino* was progressing.

Treating the *akino* like a science project helped make it feel like something outside himself. Something clinical. Impersonal. He even called himself patient X in his notes. Patient X experienced blindness. Patient X experienced a sensation he described as a drumstick stabbing into his brain. Patient X's thoughts seem to be of the morbid variety. Patient X's skin was reported to bubble after being exposed to flame.

That's what Liz had said. That his skin had *bubbled.* Patient X, Max corrected himself. A witness reported that patient X's skin had bubbled.

Max picked up the lighter again. It would be better to have a firsthand account for the file. Firsthand. Ha! A pun! Patient X still had a sense of humor. He clicked on the lighter, hesitated, then held his left index finger over the flame.

He felt warmth, but not pain. Even when he caught a whiff of something that smelled like hot dogs on a barbecue, he didn't feel any pain. And he had to agree with the witness's observation. His skin *was* bubbling.

Max lifted his thumb off the lighter, and the flame disappeared. The bubbles on his finger grew smaller, then stopped forming altogether, leaving his skin looking completely normal. No redness. No blistering. He rubbed his finger across his desk. No pain.

Fascinating. Patient X's case was truly fascinating.

Max heard a fast double knock on his door. He quickly flipped to a blank screen as Isabel barged in and flopped down on his bed.

"I've earned so many brownie points tonight, so many," she announced, smiling her most smug smile. "Everyone in Alex's family loves Isabel. The mom, the brothers. Even the dad."

"Uh, that's good," Max answered.

Even coming up with those three words was hard. Patient X was having difficulty with basic interpersonal interaction. He had to remember to write that down.

Isabel gave a sniff. "Have you been doing one of your chemistry experiments in here? It reeks. You're supposed to use the garage, remember?"

"Yeah. Forgot," he muttered.

Now was the time to tell her everything. Max had planned to tell her—and Michael, and everybody—about the *akino* yesterday night. And then again at lunch today. But he couldn't do it.

If he talked to them, he'd be talking about *he*, Max, not patient X, being about to die. He'd also be talking about his sister and his best friend, who would eventually die from the *akino,* too. Not just two more case studies to add to the file.

He couldn't deal with that. Not that.

Maybe he wouldn't have to. Maybe he would find the crystals in time. Maybe there would be a miracle cure for patient X. Maybe.

Why don't you tell Michael how you feel?

Liz had made it sound like it was no big deal. Like why don't you tell Michael that you love cats? Or why don't you tell Michael that you love horror movies? Or why don't you tell Michael that you're particularly fond of cottage cheese with raisins?

Just thinking about it—about telling Michael how she felt about him—stressed Maria out. She sat up and fumbled around on her nightstand for her little bottle of eucalyptus oil. That's what she needed right now. A walk among the calm, ancient trees, where she could forget about Liz, Michael, and everything else.

She sprinkled a few drops of the oil on her pillowcase. The scent of eucalyptus instantly filled her nose. Eucalyptus. Which, of course, reminded her of Michael.

Liz would probably say it was some kind of Freudian sprinkle, a message from Maria's unconscious telling her to get her butt out of bed and over to Michael's to confess her feelings. But Liz was a bad friend who gave bad advice. Like, for example, her all-star suggestion: "Why don't you tell Michael how you feel?"

She grabbed the phone and hit speed dial number one. Liz answered on the second ring.

"I hate you," Maria burst out without even saying hello.

"Maria?" Liz mumbled, her voice thick with sleep.

Maria shot a glance at the clock. Almost one-thirty. "Sorry, I didn't know it was so late," she said.

"But you just had to call to say you hate me?" Liz sounded equal parts confused and amused.

"Yeah. I do. I really do. How could you tell me that I should open up to Michael?" Maria knew she was talking way too fast, but she couldn't stop herself.

"So . . . so he didn't feel the same way? What did he say? Tell me everything," Liz instructed.

"He didn't say anything," Maria admitted.

"What? He just stared at you?" Liz asked.

"No, he didn't say anything because I didn't tell him," Maria answered. "I don't know if I can."

"Of course you can," Liz insisted.

"See, this is why I hate you. This is why you're a bad, bad friend. A good friend would listen to me talk about Michael a couple of hours every day and never, ever suggest that I should actually *do* anything about it."

"Slow down," Liz said. "I'm taking notes. Good friend equals wimp who only tells Maria what she wants to hear."

Maria sighed. "I'm sorry. I'm being a total lunatic. Go back to sleep."

"Wait. Just tell me one thing first. What's the worst thing that could happen if you tell Michael?" Liz asked.

Maria hesitated, running her fingers over the dozens of wrinkles in her bottom sheet. "Sometimes it's like I can feel this little glowing spot way down inside me, the place that's filled with . . . how I feel about Michael," Maria began, trying to explain her worst fear.

"With *love,* you mean," Liz interrupted.

"Fine, make me say it," Maria answered. "Loooove. Anyway, bringing up this glowing spot . . . well, it might not be pretty. I keep thinking about those fish that live way down in the ocean. When they get hooked and pulled to the surface— kablooey! Fish guts everywhere. They just explode."

"So you could explode, which I have to say is physiologically very unlikely, or, and I feel I must say this again at the risk of being a *bad, bad friend,* Michael could say he feels the same way about you," Liz said.

Her words brought a new image to Maria's mind. A picture of that little glowing piece of her rising up and exploding into a skyful of stars. Stars that shared the sky with other stars, stars from a little glowing piece of Michael.

"Well, he did kiss me twice. That's one indicator that maybe he could possibly feel the same way. Or really two indicators," Maria told Liz.

"Describe, please," Liz ordered, then gave a big yawn.

"Both were on the lips," Maria answered. "But both were really fast. And one had an element of gratitude—because I was helping him find his parents' ship. And one had an element of fear—because he thought I was practically, you know, dead. So I don't know if they really mean anything." Maria pulled in a deep breath of the eucalyptus-scented air and rushed on. "Okay, maybe they mean he doesn't think of me in a totally little sister-esque way. But they definitely don't mean Michael's looking for some kind of pledge of endless love from me."

"You're leaving out one really important fact. Michael almost got himself killed trying to save your life," Liz reminded her.

"But he probably would have done the same thing for anyone in the group," Maria answered. "Besides, if he really does feel the same way, why isn't he over here right now? Why isn't he kissing me, a real kiss that lasts more than two seconds?"

"Only one way to find out," Liz said.

"Yeah, I should just put myself out of my misery, I guess," Maria agreed. "I'm going to do it. Right now. Before I can talk myself out of it." She hung up without letting Liz say good-bye. Then she picked the phone back up and hit redial. Liz answered immediately.

"I just wanted to say that I don't really hate you," Maria announced, and then hung up again.

She climbed out of bed and crept over to her closet. She knew she had to keep moving so she wouldn't chicken out. Now the important question. "What should I wear?" she muttered. "I wonder if I have anything that goes well with exploded guts."

She gave a low growl of frustration. She grabbed her favorite pair of jeans and a nubby dark green sweater and threw them on. Then she tiptoed out of the house.

She wished she could take the car, but she was afraid the sound would wake up her mom. She pulled her bike out of the garage instead. She hesitated for a moment, standing motionless in the driveway. Maybe it would be smarter to just go back into the house and hit myself on the head with something heavy enough to knock me out for a few hours, she thought.

No, she'd gotten this far. Maria climbed on the bike and started to pedal. She decided it was a good thing she hadn't been able to drive. The pedaling gave her an outlet for all her nervous energy. Maybe she could burn most of it out before she got to Michael's. Maria pumped harder, flying down the dark streets.

It didn't take her long to reach the Pascals'. Maria jumped off her bike and laid it down next to the low hedge growing alongside the driveway. Then she hurried over to the side gate leading to the Pascals' backyard and slipped through. She circled around to Michael's window. It was open a few

47

inches. All she had to do was slide it up and crawl through.

Yeah, that was all. Plus the whole telling-Michael-she-loved-him thing.

Maria looked up at the sky. She thought maybe the stars would give her the inspiration she needed. Or the courage. Or whatever it was she needed to get herself through the last few feet that separated her from Michael.

But the sky was cloudy. Not a star to be seen. Maria turned in a slow circle. She really needed to see one star before she did this. Just one stinking star.

The window rattled up. "So are you coming in or aren't you?" a low voice asked.

Maria couldn't stop a stupid little squeak from escaping her lips. She jerked her head toward the window and saw Michael grinning at her.

"Coming in," Maria answered. "I mean, if it's okay."

Michael reached out his hand and helped her scramble inside. "Dylan's asleep, so . . ."

"No, I'm not." Dylan, Michael's thirteen-year-old foster brother, sat up in bed. "Hey, Maria."

"Hi," she whispered. Suddenly she felt like a complete idiot. This was not going to work. How was she supposed to make some romantic speech with Dylan in the next bed and Michael's foster parents asleep a couple of rooms away?

"Dylan, there's one piece of pie left. Why don't you go get it?" Michael asked softly.

"You know we have rules against eating between

meals," Dylan answered, his voice filled with indignation. Then he snickered and ducked out of the room.

Michael sat down on his bed. Maria hesitated, trying to decide if she should sit on his bed, too, or sit on Dylan's instead. Stop being such an idiot, she ordered herself, and dropped down next to Michael.

"Um, how was school?" she blurted, without looking at him.

"How was school?" Michael repeated.

"Um, yeah. I mean, are the classes a lot harder when you're a senior? Should I be worried?" Maria added.

Oh my God. *What* am I saying? Maria asked herself. She shot a glance at Michael to see if he'd started trying to make a straitjacket out of his sheet.

He hadn't. But for the first time Maria realized Michael was wearing only a pair of boxers and a T-shirt. Which didn't help the babbling problem she was having. The guy was just *too* gorgeous.

"And I was also thinking you could help me decide which electives to take next year," she rambled on. "Since, you know, you've taken some of them."

"So you came over to get advice on if you should take wood shop or choir next year?" Michael asked.

"Yes. No. I don't know," Maria said in a rush. She really wished she had the vial of cedar now. She needed to calm down—badly. She settled for a deep breath. Then she turned to face Michael. It was ridiculous to sit here talking to the wall the way she'd been doing.

"No. Definitely no. That's not why I came over," Maria said firmly, talking directly to Michael's shoulder so she wouldn't have to see the expression on his face. Then she forced herself to meet his gaze. "I came over because I never thanked you for saving my life. Thank you."

It wasn't what she'd come over here to say. But it was something she'd been wanting to tell him. And it was a big improvement over spewing about school.

"I thought you were going to die," Michael admitted, his voice husky. "I was terrified."

Then he was kissing her. Not one of those quick, friendly kisses. A hard, hot kiss, unlike anything Maria had ever experienced. It felt like that glowing piece of her was expanding, filling her whole body with heat and light. Molten heat. Blinding light. Shattering.

As suddenly as the kiss started, it ended. Michael pulled away and stared at her as if he couldn't believe what had just happened.

"I was scared you were going to die, too," Maria told him. She slid her arms around his neck and pressed her head against his shoulder. She wondered if he could feel her trembling. She wondered if he knew it was because that kiss had knocked the world out from under her feet. "It would have been my fault."

"No, don't think that," Michael mumbled into her hair.

"It's true, though," she insisted. "I should have known something bad was happening. I should have stopped using the ring. But I wanted to find it for you so badly."

"What?" Michael grabbed her shoulders and held her away from him. "You let me think what you were doing was totally safe. You kept telling me not to worry!"

"I know, but I thought . . . I thought I could find your parents' ship. I know how important it is to you, and I . . . I, um—"

"But you almost died! Why would you do that, Maria?"

"That's what I'm trying to tell you!" Maria cried. "I did it because—"

"There's no reason good enough to put yourself in that kind of danger. It has to be the stupidest thing you've ever done," Michael told her, his voice low and tight with anger.

Maria was completely unprepared for this. What happened to her plan—crawl in the window, lay her feelings on the table, and deal with the consequences? Now she felt her mind swimming through an ocean of guilt, searching for explanations. And she couldn't deal with it.

"I—I have to go," she mumbled. She pushed herself away from him and bolted to the window. Michael didn't say a word to stop her as she scrambled out and fell hard to the ground.

51

She picked herself up and ran to her bike. She climbed on and pedaled hard down the street. The wind dried her hot tears as they spilled down her cheeks.

She hadn't even gotten the chance to tell Michael *why* it was so important to her to find the ship. All she'd wanted to say was that she did it because she loved him.

"You drive, okay?" Max asked. He tossed the keys to Michael.

Michael circled around the Jeep and climbed behind the wheel. He didn't think he'd ever driven the Jeep when Max was around to drive it himself. "Are you feeling all right?" he asked.

"Yep," Max answered. "Just, I don't know, kind of tired."

Michael shot a doubting glance at Max, then turned over the ignition and pulled the Jeep out into the street. "Anyplace special you want to search?" he asked.

They had a weird role-reversal thing going on. Usually Max helped search for their parents' ship basically to keep Michael company. But tonight it had been Max's idea to go out. It wasn't even their usual day.

"I don't know. I thought we could look for that rock Maria saw when she used the Stone to track Valenti. The one she said was shaped like a chicken," Max answered.

Maria. A burst of white-hot anger blazed in Michael just thinking about what she'd done. She'd known using that stone to *see* Valenti was danger-ous, but she didn't stop. Oh no. That would be too rational. She didn't even wait until he could be with her, to watch her and make sure she was okay. The girl needed a keeper.

"Valenti was at home the first time Maria used the Stone to *see* him," Michael told Max. "Then she tried again less than an hour later. That's when she saw him drive by the rock. So we should pick a direction and head out into the desert for about forty-five minutes. Then start searching in a big cir-cle around town."

"When you say it that way, it sounds so easy," Max commented. He gave a weird, wheezing laugh.

"So, do you have a preference in direction or not?" Michael asked.

"Not," Max answered.

Michael kept the Jeep pointed straight ahead. They'd hit the desert eventually. The only bad thing about the long drive was that it gave him way too much time to think. His mind kept going back to Maria's visit to his room last night. It had com-pletely messed him up, disturbed him in so many different ways.

"I found out something you will not believe," Michael announced. "Maria *knew* she was putting herself in danger by trying to track Valenti with the ring. And she lied right to my face. She looked right at me and told me not to worry, acted like I was being overprotective."

"Hmmm," Max murmured.

"That's it? Hmmm?" Michael shook his head. "Maria, she's just not the kind of girl who lies. I mean, I can see if she got too excited about her power to be careful. But lying." He shook his head again.

"Yeah. If Maria lied, you can bet she had her reasons," Max agreed.

Michael snorted. "I guess so. She's different than Isabel. Izzy lies just to entertain herself. She's like one of those Siamese cats. You know—totally self-interested, way too beautiful, way too aware of the fact, and totally willing to use it to get what she wants."

"So if Isabel's a cat, what does that make Maria?" Max asked.

"Something in the puppy line. Like maybe a golden retriever pup. Blond and fluffy. Sweet. Eager to please."

"Advice. You might not want to let Maria in on your golden retriever analogy," Max said, then returned his attention to the search, flicking his eyes back and forth across the desert. He clearly wasn't letting anything get past him.

That was good because about one second later Michael's thoughts returned to Maria again. "I just wish I knew why she did it," he burst out. "It's driving me nuts."

In the silence that followed, Michael realized that he already knew why she did it. Maria knew if she had told him the truth, he would have made her stop using the power. And she'd wanted to find the ship so badly. That's what she'd said.

No, actually what she'd said was, "I wanted to find it for *you* so badly." For him.

He thought about asking Max if that meant Maria was . . . what, like in love with him or something. Or if it just meant they were friends, and she was looking for the ship because she wanted to help him out as a friend. No, that was way too girlie.

Bring on the barf bags.

"Is that something over there?" Max asked, his voice tense and urgent. He pointed to a rock off to the left.

Michael slowed down and studied it. "I don't think so," he answered. "It looks like your basic rock to me. Not a chicken rock."

"This is impossible!" Max cried.

"Maybe," Michael admitted. "But at least with what Maria saw, we know the ship is still intact. And we know it's been—or still is being—kept somewhere close by. We're closer to finding it than we've ever been before."

"Yeah, now it will only take us ten or twenty more years to find it," Max muttered.

Man, things must be really bad between Max and Liz again. Max was obviously having major escape fantasies. Michael knew all about those. When he was a little kid, and even not so little, he'd spent a ton of hours wishing he could find the ship, hop in, and just fly off home—with Max and Isabel, of course.

Except lately . . . lately that fantasy wasn't so appealing. Partly because now he knew for sure that he had no family back on their home planet, no one who'd be waiting to welcome him home. But it wasn't that. It was that now he had more to leave behind than he ever did before. Like Liz and Alex. And Maria.

Maria. What was he going to do about her? He'd been dancing around that question for too long. Trying to figure out if it would be just too weird to get something romantic started with her.

Romantic. Right. Translation—something physical. When he'd first started hanging out with Maria, he'd fallen into thinking of her as kind of a little sister. Even though she was the same age as Isabel, she seemed younger somehow. But it was pretty much impossible to imagine Isabel screaming through some cheesy horror movie, digging her nails into his arm, covering her eyes, and begging him to tell her when the scary part was over. Which is what Maria always did.

And he enjoyed it. But in that big brother kind of way. He wondered what would happen the next time they had one of their monster movie fests. When she hurled herself at him, would it remind him of that kiss?

That kiss. Michael sped up a little, flying into the darkness of the empty highway. He didn't know what to think about the kiss. Except that he would never, ever look at Maria as anything close to a little sister again.

"Put that you've totally fallen in love with him by reading his lists," Maria suggested. She leaned over

Isabel's shoulder as she typed. "Then sign it something like Victorianna, Mistress of the Darkness."

Maria was glad that Isabel had invited her and Liz over. She could use the distraction. Not that anything could make her stop thinking about what happened last night with Michael. But at least three percent of her brain could focus on what message to send Alex, while the other ninety-seven fixated on remembering the expression on Michael's face and the fury in his voice when he demanded to know what was wrong with her.

"Won't Alex recognize your screen name?" Liz asked Isabel.

"I'm using my mom's," Isabel answered.

Maria gave a half laugh, half snort. "What if Alex writes back? What if he tries to start some hot cybersex with your mother?"

"That is so gross," Isabel complained. "But I'm not worried. Alex is way too gaga over me to be thinking about anyone else."

"Remember that you had 'Victorianna' mention her double-D cup. And her collection of leopard-print lingerie," Liz teased. She twisted her long, dark hair into a knot at the base of her neck. "Are you still feeling so confident? Huh, Isabel? Huh, huh, huh?"

"Guys do really like big . . . collections of wild animal bras and panties," Maria added.

Isabel hit the send button and zapped the message to Alex. "Alex is completely caught in the velvet trap of my femininity," she said smugly.

Maria and Liz looked at each other and burst out laughing. "Your what?" Liz demanded.

"You heard me," Isabel answered. "So am I logging off or what?"

It would be great to be Isabel, Maria thought. So drop-dead gorgeous you could treat the world like a big guy mall. Picking up a blond here, a redhead there. Only thinking about if you wanted them, not wondering if they wanted you.

"Go to Lucinda Baker's home page," Liz said. "I want to see if there are any new entries."

"How do I get there?" Isabel asked.

"You've never gone?" Liz reached around to the keyboard and typed in the address. "It's a riot. She ranks the kissing technique of every guy in school."

Even Michael's? Maria wondered. She didn't think she wanted to read a description of Michael's kisses. What if she found out he kissed everyone the way he kissed her last night? She couldn't stand the idea that it wasn't something special that could only have happened between the two of them.

The thought of that kiss was all that was keeping her going. Yeah, Michael had seemed totally disgusted with her. Totally furious. But that kiss . . . God. That kiss gave her hope that there was a chance Michael could feel something for her. Something like love.

"Okay, here it is. You just click on a guy's name to get Lucinda's review," Liz explained.

Maria's eyes went straight to the *G*s. Michael wasn't listed. At least she was spared that.

Isabel did a fast scroll down the list. "Rick Surmacz. Interesting."

"Yeah, I thought Maggie McMahon had him caught in her velvet femininity trap," Maria joked. "How else could she get him to coordinate his outfits to hers every single day?"

Isabel gave Rick's name a click. "I call Rick the driller," she read out loud. "He somehow seems to think that a good kiss is one where he rams his tongue as far down your throat as possible. No finesse. No grace. Just gag me. Literally."

"Yowch," Maria commented. "Do you think Maggie's seen this?"

"No way," Liz answered. "If she did, the next outfit she'd pick out for him is a nice black body bag."

"Do Craig Cachopo next," Maria said, struggling to get at least four percent of her brain off Michael. "Liz and I both had a total crush on him in the sixth grade. It almost ruined our friendship."

Isabel scrolled back up the list. "He's not here," she told Maria.

"But Max is!" Liz cried. She grabbed the mouse away from Isabel and clicked.

"Okay, I shouldn't really have Max on the list because I haven't ever kissed him," Liz read, her voice losing a little of its edge. "But a girl can dream, right? And I suspect that a kiss from Max would indeed be dreamy. Those quiet types can really surprise you. Here's hoping I have some hard facts for you soon."

"Dream on," Isabel said. She gave Liz a sympathetic smile. "You've got to know that even though

Max keeps pushing you away, he has zero interest in anyone else."

Liz nodded. "Yeah, I know," she said softly. "But thanks for reminding me."

Maria felt a little stab of envy. Isabel and Liz both had these guys who were completely in love with them. Yeah, Max did insist that he and Liz couldn't be more than friends. But at least Liz knew that Max felt the same way about her that she did about him.

"Um, has Max seemed different to either of you lately?" Liz asked.

"He's been kind of out of it, if that's what you mean," Isabel answered.

Maria frowned, trying to remember how Max had been acting lately. She'd been so focused on Michael. "He's been a little quieter than usual," she offered. "Preoccupied."

"But he doesn't seem sick or anything?" Liz pressed.

"Honestly, I think it's about you. I think he misses you," Isabel told her. "That's not really the right word since you guys see each other all the time, but—"

"But it's different," Liz finished her sentence.

"If you really want to know how Craig kisses, I can tell you," Isabel announced, doing a screeching subject change. She'd obviously decided Max was not who Liz needed to be talking about. "A little wet. Some distractingly loud nose breathing. But not bad."

"No way!" Maria squealed. "I didn't know you ever went out with him."

"I didn't. But I paid him a little visit in his dreams one night. When I was, uh, campaigning for homecoming queen," she admitted. She signed off and shut down her computer.

"You went into guys' dreams and kissed them so they'd vote for you?" Liz demanded.

"Only the cute ones," Isabel answered. "And Michael and Alex totally got even with me. You'll remember that I lost to Liz." She stuck out her tongue at Liz. Liz laughed and hit her with a pillow.

Maria didn't say anything, but she was glad that Isabel had lost. It wasn't cool to win that way. Besides, Liz had deserved to win. She was as pretty as Isabel, in a completely different way. And she was just as popular.

"So what's it like, going into people's dreams?" Maria asked. "Is it really revealing? Do you know everybody's deep, dark secrets?"

"I could show you," Isabel offered. "At least I *think* I could. The three of us could form a connection, then we could go dream walking together."

"It's kind of an invasion of privacy, though," Liz said.

"Yeah. You're right," Isabel answered. "But on the other hand, it's cool."

"We have to do it," Maria jumped in.

She knew Liz was right about the invasion of privacy. But there was a chance that she could get Isabel to take her into Michael's dreams. Maybe they'd show her how he was really feeling about her.

"So, who should we do?" Isabel asked.

"Ms. Hardy?" Liz suggested.

"A teacher?" Maria asked. "Doesn't that have kind of a high *eww* factor? Maybe we should do someone we know better."

Maria didn't want to just blurt out Michael's name. She wanted to wait and do it more casually. She'd told Liz everything that happened when she went to his house. But still. She didn't want to seem desperate.

"I know. We'll go to the dream plane, and you two can each pick an orb. That way it will be a surprise," Isabel said. She sat down on the floor and motioned Liz and Maria to sit next to her. "Just relax. Breathe deeply. And I'll do the rest," she instructed. She reached out and took them each by the hand.

A swirl of color became visible around them, the deep purple of Isabel's aura, playing tag with the rich amber of Liz's, and Maria's sparkling blue. An instant later a blend of perfumes filled the air. Maria thought of them as olfactory auras. She pulled in a deep breath, savoring the distinct scents of Liz's ylang-ylang, Isabel's cinnamon, and her rose, as well as the aroma they made when they mingled.

"Close your eyes," Isabel told them softly.

Maria obeyed and found herself surrounded

by spinning globes that glistened with iridescent colors. Maria smiled as one brushed against her face. It was as soft as a soap bubble, and it was giving off one perfect note of music, high and sweet.

"Welcome to the dream plane," Isabel told them. "Each orb is created when a person begins to dream. Just pick one, and I'll take you in."

Maria strained to pick out each orb's note, searching for the one that would start up a vibration, almost an ache, inside her.

There were so many beautiful sounds, but none that she was looking for. It's because Michael isn't asleep yet, she realized. If he's not asleep, he wouldn't have a dream orb.

"You pick first," she told Liz.

"That one." Liz pointed to a whirling pale green orb.

Isabel shot Liz a look. "Freaky. I think you picked your mother's," she said. "I've done this enough to have matched up a lot of people in town with their orbs, and I'm pretty sure that's hers. Do you want to choose a different one?"

Liz hesitated, then shook her head. "That one's good."

Isabel reached out her hands and began to hum. A moment later the green orb spun into her hands. Isabel continued to hum, and the orb grew, stretching until it was as tall as they were.

"If you don't want her to see you in her dream, we can watch from out here," Isabel said. "Or we can step through and actually be in the dream with her."

"Let's stay out here," Liz answered. She took a step closer to the orb and peered inside. Maria moved up beside her.

Mrs. Ortecho was walking along the edge of a lake. As she passed under a tree, an egg tumbled out of a nest and landed at her feet. It cracked open, and blood dripped out.

Maria heard a tiny sound of distress from Liz. "We don't have to watch," Maria told her.

"No, I want to," Liz answered.

Maria returned her attention to the dream. Its scene shifted abruptly as sometimes happens in dreams, and Mrs. Ortecho was standing in a kitchen. She opened the fridge and pulled an egg out of the carton. She wrapped her hands around it, as if she was trying to give it some of her warmth.

Then instantly she was back at the lake, climbing up toward the nest with the egg still cradled in her hand. A branch broke under one of her feet. Mrs. Ortecho faltered. The egg fell from her hand, fell straight down into the lake.

The water turned red and began to bubble. And a girl shot up from the depths, drenched in blood. She flew straight at Mrs. Ortecho, her hands curved into claws.

Mrs. Ortecho screamed, and Liz jerked away from the orb. "That's enough," she exclaimed.

Isabel reached out and lightly touched the orb.

She hummed until it shrank down to its former size.

"Are you okay?" Maria asked Liz. "Pretty horrible nightmare, huh?"

"That girl. I think it was Rosa," Liz explained, her eyes glittering with emotion.

"Are you sure? I couldn't see her face with all the—" Maria stopped herself before she said the word *blood*.

Liz shook her head. "It was her," she insisted. "It's been five years since she died, five years, and my mother's still having nightmares."

"Probably only once in a while," Isabel said. "And once in a while isn't necessarily bad. Dreams help people process things."

"I guess," Liz mumbled.

Maria glanced over at Isabel. "Let's go out for a while."

Isabel closed her eyes and focused. The dream plane disappeared, and they were sitting on the floor of Isabel's bedroom once more.

"Sorry you didn't get your turn," Liz told Maria.

"It's okay. The orb I really wanted to visit wasn't there." She dropped back her head and gave a loud sigh. "I have a confession to make to you, my sister friends. I wanted to go into Michael's dream."

"Shocking," Isabel exclaimed, with exaggerated mock surprise.

Maria whirled around to look at Liz. "Did you tell Isabel?" she demanded.

"She didn't say anything. But I have eyes. And

my eyes have seen your eyes looking at Michael in *that* way," Isabel answered. She glanced at the clock. "Michael and Max and I only need a couple of hours of sleep. He won't be hitting dreamland for quite a few hours. You should stay over, both of you, and I'll take you in when it's late enough. I have pajamas and stuff you can borrow."

"I guess we could get up early enough to go home and change before school," Liz said. "But I have to call home and check," she added. Isabel reached over to her night table and pulled down the phone. She handed it to Liz, and Liz quickly punched in the number.

Maria tried not to listen. It always made her uncomfortable to hear Liz asking for permission to stay out later than planned or to go someplace outside of town. Her dad asked her a billion questions, like he didn't trust her. Which was so unfair.

Liz was an unnaturally perfect girl. Never let her grades slip. Totally responsible when she was working at the café. Did stuff around the house. Didn't drink. Didn't smoke. Didn't do any of the things that parents worried their kids were doing.

Mr. Ortecho was basically a good guy. Maria liked working for him. But she wished he'd start cutting Liz some slack. Just because Rosa had overdosed didn't mean anything like that would happen to Liz. And he should know his own daughter well enough to see that.

Liz hung up and passed the phone to Maria.

She made a quick call to her mom, who said immediately that she could stay at the Evanses'. Big surprise. Maria knew the boyfriend was over, and they were happy to have a little more private time.

"You want to watch a movie or something until it's late enough to go back to the dream plane?" Isabel asked.

"Sure," Liz answered. And Isabel started rattling off the choices.

Maria thought it was cute how Isabel tried so hard to be a good hostess. Izzy didn't have a lot of girlfriends, and it seemed as if it was really important to her to get in some good girl bonding tonight.

"Is that okay with you, Maria?" Isabel asked.

Maria hadn't been listening. Whatever movie they picked was fine by her. She thought of the movie as a countdown until it was time to go into Michael's dream orb.

By the time they'd reached the closing credits, Maria felt a whole flock of butterflies flapping in her stomach. She took Isabel's hand and again stepped into the place where the glistening, singing orbs whirled.

He'll probably be dreaming about something completely doofy, she thought. Like dancing hot dogs. Something that wouldn't have anything to do with me. Well, unless you believed some of those dream interpretation books.

Maria heard the deep sound of Michael's dream

orb. Her butterflies gave birth to more butterflies as Isabel called it over and coaxed it to expand.

Without giving herself time to do any more agonizing, Maria stepped through the soft, wet surface, Isabel and Liz right behind her.

She felt a fist tighten around her heart and squeeze. Michael definitely wasn't dreaming about dancing hot dogs. He was dreaming about having his arms wrapped around Isabel!

7

"You want help with dinner, Mom?" Max asked as he wandered into the kitchen. He knew he should be searching for the ship again, but he was too exhausted to face another discouraging drive in the empty desert.

"You can answer the doorbell when the Flying Pepperoni guy shows up. I ordered pizza," Mrs. Evans answered. "Your dad and I have a massive case we're getting ready for. No cooking time in the schedule. Lucky you."

"Not lucky Dad, though. You know what he always says—," Max began.

"He'd rather eat the box," they finished together.

Strange how much information you stored up about your parents without noticing. Useless stuff. Dad says cardboard tastes better than pizza, eats by taking one bite of each thing on his plate in sequence so he ends up with exactly one bite of everything at the end, uses three heaping tablespoons of sugar in his coffee and prefers that no one comment on it. And that was just a fragment of the information he'd collected in the *dad* file under *food*.

Max had hundreds of these mental files. Like the *Mom's childhood file*. Mom used to have an imaginary best friend named Solly, a real best friend named Annabelle, and a doll like the one Buffy had on *Family Affair*. Mrs. Beasely, that was the doll's name.

And it felt important that he knew these fun facts about his parents. Or at least that *somebody* knew it. And that somebody would go on knowing it after they were . . . gone.

But that somebody wouldn't be him. The days were clicking by—three of them already—and he could feel his body changing. And the chances of finding the ship weren't looking too good for patient X.

What was it doctors said? You should think about making arrangements. Yeah, that was it. Max had the feeling that old patient X should be making his arrangements.

And that included talking to Michael and Isabel and the others. He would have to do that. He really couldn't wait much longer.

The only good prognosis for patient X was that he was feeling less scared, less angry, just less of everything. Patient X had become a bubble boy. The moment Ray had told Max about the *akino*, it felt like a thin layer of plastic had formed around him. And every day the plastic got thicker, creating a barrier between him and everyone and everything else, even his feelings.

Maybe the oxygen in the bubble had some kind

of anesthesia mixed in with it, too. Because Max or patient X or whoever didn't care that he was a bubble boy. He didn't care that he and his mom were talking through a wall of plastic. He was having trouble caring about anything.

Strangely, though, he did sort of care about the parent information files in his head. He *would* like somebody to remember that his mother could recite that whole turnip speech from *Gone With the Wind*. That seemed important.

Max pushed himself to his feet and paced around the kitchen table, sat down, and immediately stood back up, even though his body felt like it weighed about three times as much as usual.

"How about if I make a salad?" he asked. He didn't feel like salad, but he felt like staying in the kitchen, and he might as well do something useful. He jerked open the refrigerator door and checked the vegetable crisper. There was one head of lettuce, slick with mold, and a couple of sad-looking carrots.

"I ordered us salads, too," his mother said. "So we have time for you to sit down and tell me what's wrong."

"Nothing's wrong. I just wanted to make a salad, that's all." He shut the crisper drawer with his foot and closed the fridge door.

"I'm less worried about the salad than the bags under your eyes. They're big enough for a two-week vacation. I've never seen you like this," she answered. She sat down at the table and patted the chair next to hers.

Max reluctantly sat down. He knew there was no escaping his mother when she thought they needed to talk. And it often helped. It's not that she told him what to do. It's just that a lot of times when he'd gotten through explaining whatever the deal was to her, he'd sort of figured out a solution for himself.

But there was no way that would happen this time. A long time ago he and Isabel had promised each other that they would never tell their parents the truth about their origins.

Max was going to keep that promise. If he told his parents the truth, they'd be in danger. Just like Liz, and like anyone else who got too close to him. As long as Valenti's Project Clean Slate people were hunting for aliens, everyone who knew Max, Michael, and Isabel was in danger. And that was unacceptable.

Patient X was going to die. Fine. Well, not fine, but probably inevitable. Isabel was going to die. Michael was going to die. Also probably inevitable.

But his parents didn't have to die, not for a long, long time. And he wanted to keep it that way. He wasn't going to shorten their life expectancies by telling them his secret and putting them in danger.

"So do I need to cross-examine you?" his mother asked. "Or can you bring yourself to tell me what's going on?"

He had to come up with something. His gaze drifted to the left, and he noticed one thread of gray at her temple. He reached over, plucked the hair, then held it up in front of her.

"Ow! Be kind. It will happen to you someday, too," she warned.

Actually, no, Mom, it won't, he answered silently. He slid the gray hair into his pocket. "I think I see another one," he announced. He reached for it, but his mom slapped his hand away.

"Stop stalling," she ordered.

"Okay, here's the deal," Max said. He needed a good lie, but nothing was coming to him. "Um, there's this girl at school who's totally smart and beautiful and everything. But the problem is, she keeps telling me she only wants to be friends."

Actually, he had been the one who kept telling Liz they couldn't be more than friends. It had turned out to be a good thing, too. When he died, at least she'd only have a dead friend, not a dead boyfriend.

"This makes me feel way older than the gray hair," his mother complained. "My son talking to me about relationship problems."

The doorbell rang. Max shoved himself up from the table. "I'll get it."

"Ask your dad for some money," his mom said. Then she winked at him. "You can ask him something else, too. Ask him how many times I told him I thought it would be better for us to be just friends before I finally went out with him."

Max forced himself to smile so she would think she'd made him feel better, then he headed to the front door. "Dad, I need money for the pizza guy," he yelled.

"I'm coming, I'm coming," his father called from the living room. "But couldn't we have ordered something besides pizza? I'd rather eat the box."

This might be the very last time I hear him say that, Max realized.

Michael wandered into the living room, holding a piece of cold pizza and a glass of milk.

Isabel's heart gave a hard thump, and she sloshed some of her soda onto the front of her shirt. She grabbed a napkin and blotted the spot.

"Did I scare you?" Michael asked. He flopped down on the couch next to her.

"I didn't hear you come in," she answered. He never rang the doorbell. Isabel's parents called him their third child, and he treated their home like his own.

It's true that she hadn't heard him arrive. But that's not why her heart had practically slammed a hole through her ribs. When she saw Michael, the image from his dream orb instantly flashed through her mind. And her heart had responded.

Michael stuck his feet on the coffee table, folded his pizza in half, and took a big bite. He was definitely not acting like a guy who had been dreaming about having his arms around her. In another second he'd be burping or scratching his butt.

That was a relief. It would be too weird for big brother Michael to have any kind of romantic feelings about her. Her brain knew that even if her body seemed to have temporarily forgotten.

Isabel raised her eyebrows. "Are you sure you

have everything you need?" she asked him with mock sweetness. "You want me to run upstairs and get you a few pillows or anything?"

"How nice of you to ask," Michael replied, his voice as syrupy as hers had been. "But I think I'm all set. Unless you want to take off my shoes and give me a foot rub."

"Yeah, I've really been longing to get my hands on your big, stinky feet," she answered. There was a time when she would have done it—eagerly. Back when she was, like, twelve. She'd had this major, major crush on Michael. She had an entire notebook filled with info like his favorite band and his favorite food. That notebook got fed to the garbage disposal page by page when Isabel hit thirteen and found the entries intensely humiliating.

"So, where is everyone?" Michael asked.

"My parents went back to their office. They have some humongous case. And Max is in his room. At least I think it's Max," she said. "It might be his evil twin. The one we fondly call The Mute."

"Yeah, what's with him the last few days?" Michael shoved his hands through his spiky hair. "Is it just the Liz thing or what?"

"I don't think anything new happened between them," she answered. "But maybe all that sexual frustration has gotten to be too much for him."

"Can't say that I know any." Michael smirked at her. "I'm way too good-looking to have to pay for it."

"Oh, right. I'm always forgetting that. Guess it's because I don't see it myself," she shot back.

Actually, Isabel had to admit Michael was pretty high on the yummy scale. He wasn't so much like a brother that she didn't like to look. And there was a lot to look at—black hair, intense gray eyes, those perfect six-pack abs, wide shoulders—

She stopped, suddenly feeling disloyal to Alex. Her boy definitely had it going on, too. It's just that he was lean where Michael was pumped. And sometimes pumped was fun to look at.

"Oh, speaking of your fabulous babe appeal, Corrine Williams wants me to invite you to this party she's having on Friday," Isabel told him.

"Are you and Alex going?" he asked as he stuffed the pizza crust into his mouth and wiped his hands on the legs of his jeans.

"Uh, I'm not sure," Isabel said. She wasn't looking forward to another Alex-Isabel bashing session by the Stacey crew. It wasn't fun in the locker room, and it certainly wouldn't make for a fun party.

Michael glanced at the TV. "Is this the show where she's trying to have a baby?"

He stretched his arm out along the back of the couch. It brushed against Isabel's shoulders, and she felt a tingle go through her. Which should not be happening. It hadn't happened before—at least not since she was twelve, when she was like a walking joy buzzer whenever Michael was anywhere near her.

"That's her old show," Isabel answered, sitting up a little straighter to lose the connection between her body and Michael's. "In this one she's the single mom of these two twins who are always trying to get her married."

"Oh yeah. They have witch powers or something," Michael said. "I can't believe you're watching this."

"No, that's their other old show. And I'm not really watching it. I'm watching what comes on next," she answered.

"So that guy, he's the principal of their school, right?"

Isabel shook her head. "That's *his* old show. He's their soccer coach."

"Okay, I can see that I need to be in charge of the remote," Michael announced.

He reached for it, but Isabel got there first. She held the remote behind her back.

"News flash. I'm not Alex. So I don't do that whole Princess Isabel thing," he said.

He started to reach behind her. Isabel leaned back so she was half lying on the couch and wedged the remote between her body and the cushions.

Michael studied her for a moment, his gray eyes narrowed. Another one of those tingles raced through Isabel's body, chased by a wave of guilt. She could only imagine how Maria would react if she saw this little flirt session.

"We can do this the easy way, or we can do it the hard way," Michael informed her.

"We're not doing this at all. This is my house. That means I control the remote," Isabel insisted.

"Okay. Be that way." Michael straddled her legs and started to tickle. And of course, he knew exactly the spot to go for. He'd known it for years.

Isabel squealed as he dug his fingers into her sides, right below her ribs. She couldn't take it. She grabbed him by the shoulders and shoved him away from her. At least she tried. It moved him about half an inch.

But she had other ways of winning this fight. She dug her fingernails into his back.

"Unfair. I don't have claws," Michael protested, without stopping the tickling.

"But you weigh, like, twice as much as I do," Isabel cried. "And you're practically lying on top of me."

She and Michael locked eyes, and they both froze. Isabel could feel his chest heaving. Was he just out of breath from all the tickling?

Because Isabel was sure that's why her heart had starting slamming against her ribs again. It was just because she'd been squirming around so much, trying to keep the remote away.

It had nothing to do with her sudden and intense awareness of Michael's body pressing against hers. Nothing.

Isabel pulled the remote out from behind her back and thrust it at Michael. "Here, watch what you want. I'm going to . . . go get some homework done."

8

Liz glanced at her watch. If she walked fast, she'd have time to stop at the UFO museum before her shift at the Crashdown. Good. Max would be there, and she needed to see him. Just see him and reassure herself that he was okay.

She had a bad feeling deep in her gut that he wasn't. Every day at school, he looked like more of a wreck. And there was that weird thing that happened with the Bunsen burner. Max had tried to convince her that the *bubbling* skin was just an optical illusion. But the smell of burning flesh had been too distinct.

"Liz, want a ride?" she heard a voice call from behind her. She knew without looking that it was Max.

"Great," she answered as she turned around and climbed into the Jeep.

She studied his face as he pulled back out onto the street. *He looks like a cancer patient,* she decided.

"You're staring," Max told her.

Liz decided to go for the direct approach. "I'm worried about you," she admitted. "You keep telling me nothing's wrong. But I don't buy it anymore."

"I'm just sort of tired," he told her. "I haven't been . . ."

His words trailed off. His eyes rolled up in his head until only the whites were showing.

"Max!" Liz screamed.

A long, loud horn blast yanked her attention away from him. She jerked her head up and saw a Lime Warp delivery truck about two feet away from them. They'd driven straight through a red light.

Liz reached over and jerked the wheel to the left, the Jeep's tires squealing in protest. She kicked Max's foot off the gas and pressed down on the brake, resisting the urge to slam it straight to the floor.

"Okay, okay. Now park it," she muttered to herself. She maneuvered the Jeep over to the curb and turned off the ignition, then she spun to face Max.

"Can you hear me?" she cried. She checked his eyes. Still staring white balls.

Liz swallowed hard. She had to keep it together. She had to help Max. But what should she do? She could run up to somebody's house and ask to use the phone to call an ambulance. But she didn't want to leave Max alone. Not for a minute.

"Max, come on," she shouted, her voice cracking. "Say something. Can you hear me? It's me. Liz."

His eyelids began to flutter. "Yes! That's it," Liz exclaimed. She pulled one of his hands off the wheel and rubbed it between her own. It was limp and lifeless.

She spotted a sliver of blue under his lashes,

then his eyes rolled back into place. His hand gave a twitch. He was coming out of it. Oh, thank God.

Max shook his head. "I guess I dozed off at the wheel. I've been really wiped out lately. Maybe you should drive. You can drop me at the museum, and I can get the Jeep from you later."

Liz stared at him. He was in shock. Had to be.

"Max, you had some kind of seizure," Liz said gently. "I'm taking you to the emergency room."

"To the alien section?" Max asked curtly. He slid his hand away from hers and rested it on the wheel. "Liz, you know I can't go to the emergency room. Please, just drive me home. I'll call in sick to work and take it easy, try to rest up. That's all I need. Just some rest."

"That won't make me feel much better," Liz shot back. The adrenaline was still blasting through her body. All her nerve endings felt as if they'd been electrified. And Max expected her just to drop him off at his house and cheerfully wave good-bye.

She reminded herself that he hadn't seen what she'd seen. He hadn't seen his eyes roll up and—

"Max, you've got to trust me. This isn't something you can pretend didn't happen. You've got to get yourself checked out," she told him.

"Look, I already talked to Ray about it," Max muttered. "It's not a human thing, okay? It's not a doctor thing."

Liz's stomach tightened into a twisted ball. "Then what is it? Tell me, Max."

Max ran his fingers over the grooves in the wheel.

"I need to get to work. Or at least I have to call."

Liz took his face in her hands and forced him to turn to her, but he still wouldn't meet her gaze. "We aren't going anywhere until you tell me."

"I'm dying."

Liz tightened her fingers against his face. "What?"

Finally he raised his eyes and looked directly at her.

"I'm dying."

Michael pulled the Pascals' old station wagon up behind Alex's Rabbit. He couldn't believe he'd been summoned to a meeting. The six of them saw each other every day at school. What could they possibly have to talk about that they couldn't have talked about yesterday at lunch?

He climbed out of the car and slammed the door. Whatever it was, it better be good. He was missing the game on TV. He and Dylan had a bet going, and if things went the way he thought they would, Dylan would be cleaning the toilet and polishing the bathtub in the bathroom they shared for a very long time.

Michael hurried up the Evanses' front walk and let himself in. "I hope you didn't get me over here because you've decided we need uniforms in the colors of our auras or something," he complained as he stepped into the living room. "Because if you did—"

His throat closed up around his words as he saw Max's grim face. Something was very wrong.

Michael dropped into the closest chair. "What?" he asked softly.

Max didn't answer. Michael jerked his gaze to Liz. Her eyes were red, and faint tear tracks ran down her cheeks. "Somebody start talking. Now. Is it Valenti? Did he find out something?"

"They haven't told us anything yet," Maria said. "They were waiting for you." She looked as scared as he felt. So did Alex and Isabel.

"Well, I'm here now." He leaned forward, his eyes locked on Max again.

"I . . . we . . ." Max cleared his throat. He shoved his hair away from his face, and Michael could see his fingers trembling. "There's something called an *akino*. It's . . ." His words trailed off.

"The *akino* is something everyone from your planet goes through. It's their time to connect to something called the collective consciousness." Liz spoke up, glancing from Isabel to Michael and back again. "Ray said that it contains all your civilization's knowledge, all the emotion, too. It basically lets you feel the emotions of everyone on your planet all at once. Maybe even the ones who have died. I'm not sure."

Liz lowered her gaze to the coffee table, and Michael thought he could see new tears welling up in her eyes. He felt like springing up and shaking her until she finished her thought. He gripped the arms of the chair as hard as he could to keep himself in place.

"Come on, Liz," Isabel begged.

Liz pulled in a deep, shuddering breath. Then the words began tumbling out of her mouth so quickly, it was difficult to make them out. "Max is going through the *akino,* and that means he has to connect to the collective consciousness or he'll die. But he can't connect to the consciousness from earth without the communication crystals from your parents' ship."

This had to be a joke. Like a week ago, Michael found out from Ray that his parents were dead. He also found out that he had no family at all back on his home planet. And now . . . now his best friend was dying? This had to be a sick joke.

Michael heard Isabel begin to whimper low in her throat. The sound ripped through him. A cry like that should never be coming out of Isabel. She sounded like an animal who had been caught in a trap for days, hopeless, in pain, dying.

Dying. And it would happen to all of them. Soon Isabel would be dying, too. And by then he and Max would probably have already died. Leaving his Izzy to go through it all alone.

"How long?" Michael demanded, breaking the heavy silence.

"Ray said—," Liz began.

"Months, weeks, or days," Max interrupted, sounding as if he was forcing the words through a barrier at the back of his throat. "I don't know how long until you or . . . I don't know when it will start. I guess it happens at different times for different people. It could be years." He locked eyes with Michael briefly, then his gaze skittered away.

It could be tomorrow, Michael thought, filling in what Max had left unsaid.

"So we need a plan to find the ship," Alex said. Maria joined in, babbling about notes and maps and stuff.

What was wrong with them? Michael thought. He'd been searching for that ship his entire life. The chances of finding it in the next couple of days were slim. Unless . . . Michael remembered that Ray said he had hid the Stone of Midnight in the cave. Hmm . . .

He straightened up and saw Liz staring at him with a tiny half smile on her face.

"I have an idea," she said slowly.

Alex and Maria kept jabbering. "Let Liz talk," Michael ordered.

"I have an idea," she repeated. "I was just sitting here, looking at Michael, and suddenly I remembered how we saved him from the bounty hunters."

"We all made the connection!" Maria exclaimed. "And it was strong enough to bring him back. Why didn't I think of that! When the six of us connect, it's . . . I don't even have a word for it."

Liz turned to Max. "Maybe the strength of our connection would give you enough of a boost to complete the *akino* without the crystals. What do you think?"

Michael knew what he thought. He thought it was a monumentally better idea than trying to find the ship in time. And if it didn't work, he would go to the cave and solve this thing himself.

The strength of the connection had saved his life. Why shouldn't it be able to save Max's, too?

Max reached out and took Liz's hand in his left and Isabel's in his right, completing the circle. The connection crackled between the six of them instantly.

This time their auras were like spears of laser light, slashing across the Evanses' living room with an electric sizzle. Shooting out sparks where the six blades of light crossed in the center. There, in the heart of the circle, the six individual colors blazed in a ball of bright white light. His emerald green, Michael's brick red, Maria's sparkling blue, Liz's warm amber, Isabel's rich purple, and Alex's bright orange combined into that one blinding light.

The hair on Max's arms stood up as the strength of his friends blasted into him, turning his veins to live wires. It felt as if they were each directing their *essence* toward him. He laughed as Alex zapped him an image of Popeye's muscles bulging after a can of spinach, then gasped as Liz showed him a flock of exotic parrots all taking flight at once. The images came faster and faster. Isabel showing herself hitting him with a shovel during a fight when they were kids. A shark, dead eyes and razor teeth torpedoing through the water from Michael. A flower going from blossom to full bloom in seconds from Maria.

An instant later the music rang out. One note for each of them. Each note a different frequency, each setting up its own vibration along his glowing veins.

He felt invincible. Every sense was filled with their connection. The colors of their auras, the sound and feel of their music, the emotion of their images, and the scents, the scents were exploding in his nose—the rose, the cedar, the eucalyptus, the ylang-ylang, the cinnamon, and the almonds. He pulled in a deep breath, drawing the perfumes deep into his lungs, into each tiny air sac.

Now, he told himself. *Now!*

He reached out with his mind, searching for a glimmer, a whisper, something to give him a direction. He squeezed his eyes shut, trying to send a little part of him, of *them,* out into the universe. Past the edges of the galaxy. Deep into the silence of space.

He felt his body go weightless. Light, so light. As if it had been converted into pure electricity, streaking past planets that had no name. He could almost see them rushing by.

Somewhere out there was the combined psyche of every person who had lived on his planet. Somewhere out there was a living record of every thought, every emotion, every dream. He had to be able to feel that.

I'm here. I want to join you. I want to connect. Max

tried to hurl the message out in front of him, throw it across the void.

Suddenly Max thought he heard an answer. As light as a single strand of hair slipping across his face, he thought he felt another mind, or minds, brush against his. He didn't get an image, or a sound, or a scent. But still, he'd felt the touch of something not him. Something from outside the group.

Yes! He shouted the word inside his head. *Yes! I want to join you. I need to connect. I have reached my* akino.

At the word *akino* the sound of a million voices filled Max's head. A million voices all speaking at once, all demanding his attention, shrieking louder and louder as they fought to be heard.

Jangled notes of music, with no rhythm, no order, rose over the voices, sending shock waves through his eardrums.

Images of faces, animals, plants rushed through his mind. Deaths, births. Wars, famines, celebrations. Formulas, schematics, equations.

Max could feel the blood begin to rush through the arteries and veins of his brain as he struggled to take it all in. He could feel the vessels swelling, gorged with the blood. Bursting.

He could actually feel the synapses firing their electric currents. Firing again and again, trying to keep up with the demands of all the information. Electrifying his brain.

Max stretched open his mouth and screamed.

He thought he heard the others screaming, too—Liz, Michael, Isabel, Alex, and Maria. Screaming for it to stop.

Then all was blackness.

The next thing he heard was a voice. One single voice.

"We have to stop meeting like this."

Max opened his eyes and saw Ray Iburg staring down at him with both his hands pressed against Max's forehead. "All better?" he asked.

Max did a quick self-inventory. He actually felt pretty good. Or as good as he'd been feeling since the *akino* began. "Yeah. Thanks. How did you know to come?"

"The shout of pain I heard wasn't exactly subtle," Ray answered. He moved over next to Liz and placed his hands on her forehead.

Max swept the circle. Everyone had been knocked out cold. "Let me help," he told Ray, starting to slide over to Isabel.

"Park it," Ray ordered. "I don't want to have to heal you twice. What were you all trying to do, anyway?"

"We were trying to help Max connect to the collective unconscious," Liz mumbled. She sat up, and Max could see that the color was already returning to her face. Ray did good work.

"I'm lucky I didn't find a big vegetable patch when I showed up," Ray told them as he placed his hands on Michael. "Another few seconds and you would have been about one IQ point above rutabagas. And I don't know if I'd have been able to get you back."

"Guess that would make for an interesting valedictorian speech from you, huh, Liz?" Michael asked. "A rutabaga's thoughts on what to expect after grad."

"Yeah. Many exciting avenues are available, fellow graduates. Salads, soups," Liz muttered. "Rabbit food."

Alex sat up and blinked a couple of times. "So I guess we should start making plans to search for the ship."

Max gave a harsh bark of laughter. "Maybe we should wait until Isabel and Maria have regained consciousness," he said.

"I guess," Alex answered. "But it's not like you . . . It's not like we have a lot of time."

Michael pressed a cold Lime Warp can against his head and pretended to listen to the plans for that night's search parties. He didn't have to do more than pretend to listen because he'd already decided that search parties were useless. They had to use the Stone of Midnight.

Correction. *He* had to use the Stone. He'd use it to watch Valenti and find the ship. And if using the Stone brought the bounty hunters down on him again, well, today was a good day to die. A friggin' perfect day. As long as he could get the ship's location first. As long as he could save Max and Isabel.

93

Of the three of them, he was the best choice to make the sacrifice. Max and Izzy had a family. Their parents would be destroyed if anything happened to either of them.

It wasn't like that for Michael. It's not as if the Pascals cared that much about him. Yeah, the group . . . they would miss him. But they'd still have each other. Izzy would still have Max. She wouldn't be left alone.

"What do you think, Michael?" Alex asked.

"Three teams of two. Plus Ray on his own. Fine," he answered. He was pretty sure that's what they had just suggested. He just wanted this meeting of theirs to end so he could get out to the cave. He'd stashed the Stone out there. That pen he lifted off Valenti's desk, too.

"So we start tonight?" Maria asked.

"Yeah. Let's meet at the school parking lot at seven," Isabel said.

No one objected to that plan, so Michael sprang to his feet. "I'll see you all there," he said as he hurried out of the room. By the time he made it through the front door, he was running. He climbed into the wagon and headed out of town, careful to keep his speed down. Valenti loved to stop teenagers, and Michael didn't have the time.

Michael focused all his attention on getting to the cave. Anytime a thought about Max weaseled its way into his brain, he shoved it right back out. He didn't need to think about Max, worry about Max, cry over Max. None of that. Because he was taking care of the situation. Right now.

Michael turned off the highway and muscled the station wagon across the desert. He pulled to a stop about half a mile from the cave. He didn't want anyone—like someone from Project Clean Slate— wondering what the wagon was doing out there and then poking around.

Michael jumped out of the car and sprinted to the cave. Taking care of it, taking care of it, taking care of it. The words pounded through his head in the rhythm of his footfalls.

When he reached the crack in the desert floor that opened into the cave, he swung himself down in one easy motion. Without hesitation he headed straight to the corner where he kept his sleeping bag. The ring with the Stone set in it was in the bottom. So was the pen.

Michael crouched down and pulled them out. He jammed the ring on his finger and clutched the pen in his hand. "Okay, where's Valen—"

"Don't do it, Michael!"

He heard a scrabbling sound and Maria half jumped, half fell into the cave. She stumbled to her feet and raced toward him. She knocked the pen out of his hand and sent it flying.

"What the hell are you doing here?" he demanded.

"I followed you," she shot back, her blue eyes blazing. "Not that I needed to. The second you stood up from your chair, I knew where you were going." She pulled in a gasping breath and rushed on. "What is wrong with you? That's what you asked me when you found out I kept using the Stone when I knew it was dangerous. Now you're doing the same thing. So now I'm asking you. What is wrong with you?"

"It's not the same." Michael strode across the cave and snatched up the pen. "I'm using the Stone to find the ship so I can save Max's life. Save his *life*. That's what's wrong with me, Maria."

"No, I'll tell you what's wrong. The bounty hunters are going to come after you again . . . and this time they're going to kill you!" Maria yelled.

"So what?" Michael asked. "That means two alive, one dead. Not three dead, the way it will be if I don't use it."

"Oh, fine. I should have thought of that. Two out of three. That's great," Maria answered, tears choking her voice. "Now I have no problem with you killing yourself."

Great. She was crying. Really crying, the sobs shaking her whole body. He took a step toward her.

"No!" she exclaimed. "Don't come over here. And don't try to touch me! I don't want you to touch me when you're just going to kill yourself the second I go away. Don't . . ."

Maria covered her face and broke down. Michael shifted his weight from one foot to the other. Her hysterical sobs grew louder.

He couldn't take it anymore, just standing and watching. He hesitated another moment, then crossed the distance between them in three long strides. He reached for her, but she lowered her hands quickly, and the expression on her face stopped him.

"I meant it—don't touch me," she said. She wiped her eyes with her sleeve, then pulled a tissue out of her pocket and blew her nose.

"Are you okay?" he asked. "I'm sorry I yelled at you. It's just . . . there's not much time."

"You think you're being some kind of hero, don't you?" Maria asked, only the slightest tremble remaining in her voice. "But you're not. You're being selfish. You get to feel so good about yourself for being the big man, making the sacrifice. You're not even thinking about how Isabel or Max would feel."

"I don't care how they'd feel. At least they'd be alive to feel *something*," Michael said harshly.

"Try to think how you'd feel if Max gave up his life for you," Maria answered. "Or Isabel. Think about how it would really feel if Isabel sacrificed her life to save yours."

Michael couldn't answer that. He couldn't get close to imagining how he'd feel. His mind kept leaping away from the thought.

"They love you," Maria said softly. "Everything you feel for them, they feel for you. I know you think they have each other and their parents, so they can't possibly care about you the way you care about them since you have no one. But it's not true."

Michael felt tears sting his eyes, and he blinked them away fast.

"Alex and Liz, they love you, too. Something else for you to deal with," she added. "Anything you do to hurt yourself hurts us. If you let the bounty hunters kill you, it would kill us. It would kill *me*." She looked up at him. "Because I love you, too. I love you, Michael."

She wasn't saying she loved him as a friend. She was saying she *loved* him loved him. Whoa. He didn't even know what to do with that.

Maria reached out and slid the ring off his finger. He let her.

"So, is it okay if I touch you now?" he asked.

"Just don't mess up my hair," she answered.

He choked out a laugh and wrapped his arms around her.

"We'll find the ship," Maria promised him. "All of us. Together. We can do anything."

Michael didn't answer. He just pulled her even closer and held on tight.

"Can't you go any faster?" Isabel demanded. She was sure Michael had decided to use the Stone. She never should have let him walk out of the house. It's just that the movie screen inside her head showed Max lying in a coffin, his face pale except for garish smears of makeup. And the coffin being lowered into the ground by a creaking metal cable.

Isabel squeezed her eyes shut as the images flooded her again. It didn't help. Eyes open or closed, the movie filled her vision. The movie's odorama was working fine, too. She could smell the dirt and the thick, cheap blush.

"If we get pulled over, it will take us a lot longer to get there," Alex answered. But he goosed the accelerator a little.

"Okay, you're right." Isabel turned and stared out into the desert. But the movie of Max's funeral kept running. And then the theater in her mind became a multiplex. One screen still showed Max being lowered into the ground. One showed Michael using the Stone and then collapsing. One showed a classic—her old boyfriend Nikolas being shot by Sheriff Valenti.

And one showed Isabel standing alone in a flat, endless, snow-covered field. All alone in the frigid, silent whiteness. All alone until it was finally her turn to die.

She shot a glance at Alex. She knew if she told him what was in her mind right now, he'd say that no matter what happened, she wouldn't be alone. He would be right there with her, to comfort her, to warm her.

But it wasn't the same. Max and Michael, and even Nikolas, shared a bond with her that was stronger than anything she could possibly share with Alex. The bond of identity, and powers, and species memories. The bond of living in a world where you were hunted.

To have all those bonds severed would be like standing in that field. The movie Isabel opened her mouth wide and screamed. Only an echo answered her.

If it seemed as if Max was going to die, Isabel would go after Valenti. She didn't need the Stone to find out what she needed to know. She would use her mind to squeeze his pathetic excuse for a heart until he squealed like a pig and told her everything she wanted to know.

If he ended up dying, fine. It was a lot better than Max dying. Or Michael. Or her.

"Almost there," Alex told her as he pulled off the road. The Rabbit bumped and jerked as they sped across the hard-packed sand of the desert. "Looks like Maria beat us to it."

He was right. That was definitely Maria's mom's car, which she'd driven over to the Evanses'. It was parked right next to the Pascals' wagon. Isabel felt a pang of jealousy that Maria had found Michael first, then a pang of guilt for her jealousy.

"How did she know to come here?" Isabel asked.

"Same way you did, I guess," Alex answered.

Alex parked next to the other two cars. He and Isabel climbed out and started toward the cave. Alex slid his arm around her shoulders as they walked. Isabel wished he hadn't. It felt too heavy. Not warm-and-reassuring heavy. More a slowing-her-down heavy.

She knew that Maria had probably stopped Michael from using the Stone. But she wanted to see for herself. "Let's run." She broke away from Alex and pounded toward the cave. She scrambled down, feeling for the big rock with her toes.

A quick scan of the cave showed her that

Michael was fine. It also showed her that he had his arms wrapped tight around Maria, his face buried in her hair.

Right now, that's where Isabel wanted to be. In Michael's arms.

Alex rushed up behind her. He slid his arm around her waist and pulled her tight against him. "See? It's okay. We made it in time."

Isabel nodded. But she couldn't help wishing they'd arrived a few moments earlier. At least a few seconds before Maria and Michael ended up wrapped around each other.

"Max, you and Liz take this section here." Michael pointed to a quadrant of desert on his worn map.

"Got it," Max answered. He kind of wished Michael hadn't paired him up with Liz, though. Liz was the one person who'd been able to penetrate his plastic bubble. This afternoon, when she'd held his face in her hands and insisted that he tell her about the *akino*, a big piece of his protective coating had been torn away. When he was with her, he was a hundred percent Max, not the anonymous patient X.

It had felt good to tell her the truth. But it'd hurt, too. Almost more than he could bear.

"My name is Liz, and I'll be your chauffeur tonight," she told him. She tried to say it in a joking way, but he could tell the memory of his seizure, or whatever it was, was still raw in her mind.

Max tossed her the keys as they headed to the Jeep. "It's always been a fantasy of mine to have, well, not a female chauffeur—more like a female butler," he answered. He wasn't all that much better than Liz at hitting a jokey tone.

"You know, someone who does everything Alfred does for Batman but who does it while being a young, hot female instead?" Alex called after them, a hint of strain in his voice, too.

"Exactly," Max replied. He hoisted himself into the Jeep, trying to make the movement look easy, although it really took some effort now. One of the hundreds of little things that were becoming harder every day.

"You going to put your seat belt on?" Liz asked after she snapped hers in place.

"What's the point?" he asked, without thinking. Then he heard Liz's sharp intake of breath, and he quickly strapped himself in. This keeping-up-normal-appearances thing was trickier than he realized.

Liz turned the Jeep around and headed out the south driveway. About twelve minutes later they were alone on the highway, heading into the desert.

"I forgot how hard it would be to find that chicken rock Maria described now that it's dark," Liz commented.

"Michael, Isabel, and I can see better at night than during the day," Max reminded her. "It's good we divided the teams the way we did."

Except he probably would have preferred being matched up with Alex or Maria. Just sitting next to Liz, now that she knew the truth, poked more holes in his bubble. The feelings, the sorrow, the fear, the anger were finding ways in. And the anesthesia wasn't working quite so well.

Maria peered into the desert, searching for anything that looked familiar from *seeing* Valenti that night. It was so hard to tell. A lot of the desert looked like . . . the desert.

She wished she'd been paired up with Max instead of Michael. Being in the car with him was giving her the sweats, and she was trying to remember if she'd put on herbal deodorant before she rushed over to the Evanses' this morning. So much had happened since this morning.

Including Maria finally telling Michael she loved him. She took a quick peek at him from under her lashes. He was totally focused on scanning the desert as he drove. She had a feeling she could be sitting there naked and he wouldn't notice.

What was he thinking? Was he totally freaked out by what she said? Yeah, he'd hugged her. But he definitely hadn't said, "I love you, too." Maybe he would have if Isabel and Alex hadn't shown up. Then again, maybe he was too preoccupied with saving his best friend's life, Maria told herself.

A long, pissed-off-sounding horn blast jerked her out of her thoughts. She glanced over her shoulder and saw a beat-up Caddy riding on their tail.

"It doesn't occur to him just to pass us?" Michael complained. "It's not like there's not room. Nothing but room out here."

The guy in the Caddy gave another long honk. Maria turned around and waved for him to pass them. The guy didn't look at all appreciative. He looked royally—

Familiar. Familiar from when she *saw* Valenti.

She tried to picture him with a machine gun strapped across his chest. "Michael, I think that's the guard from the compound where the ship is kept," she told him, her voice shaking with excitement. "Can you get me a better look?"

Michael angled the station wagon over to the shoulder. As soon as the Caddy passed them he pulled up alongside it so that Maria was even with the driver's side window. "If this is him, we won't need to worry about any chicken rock. He can lead us right there," Michael said.

The guy in the caddy rolled down his window. "Oh, now you want to go fast," he yelled. "Great."

Maria felt as if she'd stepped on an elevator shooting straight down. She was wrong. "No, the guard was a lot younger," she told Michael. "Sorry."

Michael dropped back, and the Caddy roared off. "Guess that would have been a little too easy," he muttered.

Maria felt like reaching over and touching his shoulder or his arm, just some little touch so that he knew he wasn't alone in all this. But she kept her hands locked in her lap and changed her focus to the task at hand.

Maria pressed her forehead against the cool glass of the window and tried to concentrate every bit of her attention on finding the rock, checking the shape of every one she saw. Not-chicken. Not-chicken. Not-chicken.

About a hundred not-chickens later, Michael

pulled into the desert and stopped the car. "Did you see something?" she cried.

"No, I *felt* something. A burst of fear," he answered.

"From Max or Isabel?" Maria demanded. She knew that the aliens could feel each other's emotions. Michael shook his head.

"Then who? Oh, Ray. How strong was it? Do you think he's okay? Should we go find him?" Maria asked in a rush.

"Wait. Let me focus a minute," he answered.

Maria held perfectly still, the sound of her own breathing loud in her ears.

"I don't know who it is." Michael sounded amazed . . . and disturbed.

"How can you be sure what you felt isn't from Ray or Max or Isabel?" Maria asked. "It's just raw feeling, not thoughts or anything, right? All three of them have to be having pretty extreme emotions right now. Maybe that's why it feels different."

"It's, I don't know how to describe it. It's like different people have different flavors," Michael answered. "I don't recognize this one. It's not from anyone familiar."

"Flavors?" Maria repeated.

"I can't explain it better than that," he told her. "It's not something you can really understand if you haven't experienced it."

Maria nodded. I bet Isabel would understand, she thought. Is he wishing she was here with him right now?

*   *   *

"Wait." Alex pulled the Rabbit to a screeching halt. "Does that look like a chicken to you?" He pointed to a rock off to the left.

"That?" Isabel squinted. "A frog, maybe. Aren't frog legs supposed to taste like chicken?"

"You're looking at it from the wrong angle." He pulled her closer to him, breathing in her spicy perfume. "See, it's like a chicken pecking the ground. That's its beak."

"You're right." A huge smile broke across Isabel's face. "You're right! I think we found the chicken rock!"

Alex threw open his door, and they both raced over to the rock. It looked even more like a chicken up close. He hadn't been expecting to find it the first time out. He'd had his doubts that they'd find it at all. But here it was! The chicken rock! He let out a loud cluck and started beating his arms like wings. Isabel started clucking, too, and scratching her foot against the ground. They circled each other, clucking, pecking, scratching, and laughing. He was laughing so hard, his sides started to cramp. But he didn't care.

Max was going to live! Isabel was going to live! Michael was going to live!

Alex stopped clucking and grabbed Isabel. He swooped her off the ground and spun them both in fast, dizzying circles. He was obviously in the midst of some stress/relief-from-stress hysteria. But he didn't care! It felt too good.

"Put me down," she half laughed, half gasped.

He reluctantly slid her to the ground. She spun in one more slow circle, her laughter trailing off, her smile disappearing.

"What? We found the chicken rock! Yeah!" he cried.

"But where's the compound?" Isabel asked. "I don't see anything but desert."

"Maybe underground?" Alex offered, starting to feel idiotic for getting excited over a rock. It wasn't celebration time yet. "We should look for cracks in the desert floor, like the entrance to your cave."

"You can't see the cave entrance until you're practically standing on top of it. And we have no idea how far Valenti drove past this rock," Isabel answered. "This is totally hopeless."

"No, it's not. We'll get everyone out here. Concentrate the search," Alex argued, trying to convince himself as much as he was her.

"It's still going to take too long." Isabel's voice rose into a shriek. She clasped her hand over her mouth as if she couldn't believe that sound had come out of *her*. "Sorry," she muttered.

"Don't be sorry," Alex reassured her. "I understand."

"You can't understand," she said quietly, without meeting his gaze. "I know you want to. I even know you try. But you *can't*."

"That's it. We've covered our assigned section." Liz turned the Jeep around and headed back toward town.

Max's eyes felt tired from the strain of staring out into the desert. He let them drift up to the stars. They were so bright, so close to the earth. He found the sight of them soothing somehow.

"A lot of them are part of binary pairs," Liz commented, catching him stargazing. "Even through a telescope they can still look like a single star. Things . . . they just seem to belong in twos," Liz continued.

He made an oh-interesting kind of noise, without turning toward her. He wasn't liking the way this conversation was going.

"What happened to you, it's made me think about the just-friends thing." Liz suddenly pulled the Jeep off into the desert and stopped.

"We need to get back," Max said. He lowered his gaze from the sky but still didn't look at Liz. If she tried to make him talk about how he felt about her, he would lose it. The bubble would get ripped away all at once, leaving him defenseless. Skinless.

"This is important," she insisted, getting that stubborn sound in her voice. "When you told me we had to be just friends, you said it was for my own protection."

"It was, it is," Max answered, without looking at her. "Getting too close to me can bring Valenti down on you—you know that. And you know what he's capable of. He killed Nikolas right in front of us."

"I know," she told him. "That's not my point. My point is that you've been keeping us apart because you wanted me to be safe. But it's you who . . . who are in danger right now. Not from Valenti. Not from anything you even knew existed."

"But what does that have—," he began to protest, finally turning to face her, struck as always by how beautiful she was with her sleek hair, perfectly formed lips, and dark eyes.

"I'm trying to explain. Just listen," she said.

Just listen. As though that was nothing. As though her words weren't slicing through his heart.

"We don't know what is going to happen to either of us," she went on. "You could get hit by a car before your *akino* even reaches its . . . conclusion. I could get leukemia or something. Neither of us knows how much time we have. I just want to know why you won't let us be together for whatever time we do have. Why, Max?"

Max tilted back his head and stared up at the stars. How could he answer that? How could he explain something that hardly made sense even to him anymore?

"I wonder which ones are pairs," he said, stalling.

"We are," she answered softly. "We shine with the same light."

He lowered his head and looked at her again. "You're right," he admitted. "But what if—"

"Shhh." Liz unfastened her seat belt and leaned toward him until her lips were just a fraction away from his. He could feel their warmth across the tiny distance.

All he had to do was make one infinitesimal

move. How could he turn away from her? Max closed the distance with the softest kiss. Everything about this moment felt fragile, as if one wrong breath could shatter it.

Then Liz wrapped her arms around him, squeezing onto the seat beside him, and he realized he was wrong. There was nothing fragile here. Liz was strong, and warm, and vitally alive.

He wanted to get closer to her, even closer. He slid his hands under her shirt and ran them up the smooth skin of her back. Liz twisted around, trying to bring more of her body in contact with his. She deepened their kiss, inviting his tongue into her mouth, stroking it with hers.

A low groan escaped from his throat. Then Liz let out a yelp of pain.

Max broke their kiss. "What happened?" he exclaimed.

"I cut my hand. On the roll bar, I think. There must be a rough rivet or something," she answered.

"Let me see." He took her hand and studied it. "It's pretty deep. Let me heal it for you."

"It's like the day in the café," she said.

The day he had healed her gunshot wound. The day he had trusted her with his secret. The day everything had changed forever. Pretty much the best and worst day of his life. Until today. It was worse, but better, too.

Max took a deep breath and focused on making the connection he would need to heal the gash. Instead of the rush of images from Liz he expected, he got the same one again and again—the image of him with his eyes rolled back in his head.

Why wasn't it working? Why wasn't he in? Max took another breath. Think of Liz, he told himself. But he only got the same sickening image.

Liz eased his hand away from hers. "It's okay. It's no big deal. Do you have a handkerchief or something? We can just make a bandage."

Max ripped the bottom off his T-shirt and carefully wrapped it across her palm. "Will you be okay to drive?" he asked.

"Yeah." She slid back behind the wheel and pulled back onto the highway. The desert around them felt much darker and dangerous now, now that he knew he no longer had his powers.

"Looks like we're the last ones back," Alex commented as he pulled into the school parking lot.

Isabel didn't answer. He hadn't really expected her to. She'd been silent the whole drive back. So had he. Every time he thought of something to say, he remembered Isabel insisting that he couldn't understand. And whatever brilliant comment he'd come up with seemed way too lame to say.

He parked next to Max's Jeep, and they hurried over to the others. "We found the chicken rock," he announced. "But no sign of the compound," he added quickly before they could all start dancing and clucking.

"At least we're a little closer," Maria said. She pulled the sleeves of her sweater down over her hands, like she was freezing or something. Alex didn't think it was *that* cold out.

"If you want to assign us areas to search around the rock, I'm definitely up for going back out there," he told Michael.

Liz shot a look at Max. "Why don't we meet up here tomorrow morning instead?"

Alex took another glance at Max, trying not to be

too obvious about it. Yeah, he looked about ready to topple. "Tomorrow's good for me," Alex answered.

"I was thinking we could hit the party at Corrine Williams's," Michael suggested. "It will have heated up pretty nicely by now."

"Do you want to?" Alex asked Isabel. He figured a little distraction might be good. He wondered if she was thinking much about what the *akino* info meant to her directly. Or if she was only thinking about Max right now.

Alex was definitely trying to keep his brain on the Max problem. If he started to think about Michael and Isabel . . . if he started to think about them dying, too, he'd end up getting himself locked in a loony bin somewhere.

Isabel also checked Max's face. "I think I'd rather just go home."

"You're all going to the party," Max insisted. "What, do you think I want you all sitting around staring at me?"

"I like staring at you. Please, please, let me come over and stare at you," Liz half teased.

"No, I want you to go, too. It sounds like fun," he told her. "I just want to go home and crash."

"Okay, then it's settled. We can all go in my car. Her whole street's probably going to be jammed," Alex said.

"I'll drop Max home and then meet up with you," Liz promised.

They all stood there for a second, then Michael started toward Alex's car and Alex, Isabel, and

Maria fell in behind him. Alex blasted the radio the second he slid in the driver's seat so they wouldn't have to try and make conversation.

He was relieved when he parked at the end of Corrine's block. The party had spilled out onto the lawn. It was still in the packed, loud, noisy phase. Perfect.

Alex slid his arm around Isabel's shoulders as they started down the street. He felt her tense a little when he touched her. "You okay?" he whispered.

She nodded and slipped her arm around his waist, twisting her fingers around one of his belt loops. Alex got another one of those piggish bursts of look-at-the-girl-who's-with-me pride, especially as he cut across Corrine's front yard and headed inside.

He noticed that he and Isabel were getting quite a few looks. And it felt pretty good, he had to admit. "I'll get us drinks," he yelled in her ear. There was no point in both of them fighting their way into the kitchen.

She smiled at him, one of those full-out goddess-Isabel-is-smiling-on-you smiles. For one moment it pushed everything else out of his mind. Everything.

He started elbowing his way into the kitchen, unable to keep the big, dorky smile off his own face.

"Have I slipped into an alternate universe?" a guy yelled from behind him. "Because I just saw Isabel Evans walk in here with that guy Alex from gym. I thought she only went out with college studs and basketball stars. . . ."

*   *   *

117

Michael leaned against the willow tree in the far corner of Corrine's backyard. He had thought he wanted to come to the party, but he'd forgotten about the Maria factor.

He was still reeling from what she said to him in the cave.

It was just too much, too quick. He didn't know what he was supposed to do now. If he went inside and she came over to him, was he supposed to dance with her? Driving around in the car with her was hard enough. But dancing. Touching. How could you do something like that after a girl said she loved you? Wouldn't she think it meant something? Didn't girls always think everything *meant* something?

What he really wanted was for things to go back the way they were. Where they could just hang together, have fun, watch bad movies.

Okay, maybe he'd like things back the way they used to be with some kissing added in. Now that he had the whole little sister issue out of the way forever, he would like to be able to kiss Maria once in a while.

But he didn't think he wanted some big, intense, Max-and-Liz tragic love thing. And the way Maria looked at him when she told him she loved him—it didn't get any more big and intense than that.

"Stacey said you had to bring Michael *and* Max to make up for Alex," Corrine said into Isabel's ear.

Stacey said. She wondered how many of the Staceyettes were going to come over and tell her what Stacey said. Probably every single squealing,

118

giggling one of them. It's what they lived for.

She so did not need this tonight.

"And where's your date?" Isabel pretended to search the crown. "Is he blowing chunks in the bathroom? Or has he passed out already?"

"He had to leave early," Corrine answered. Then she rushed away.

I'll bet he did, sweetie, Isabel thought. She spotted Alex coming out of the kitchen and made her way over to him. She took the drinks out of his hands and set them on the floor by the wall.

"Let's dance first," she said. She grabbed Alex's hand and pulled him over to a tiny open space near where Doug Highsinger was dancing with Stacey. She wanted Stacey to see that she wasn't slinking around, looking like she had something to hide.

Alex put his hands on her waist, and they started to sway to the music. Isabel arched her spine and leaned back, making sure her hair brushed across Doug Highsinger's bare arm. When he looked, she did a slow, graceful return into Alex's embrace, stretching herself against his body.

She didn't need to look to know Dougie kept his eyes on her the whole way. Take that, jerk-off, she thought. He'd been panting after her since junior high, but she hadn't gone out with him ever.

Yep. He had to settle for Stacey. Isabel smiled as she slid her hands through Alex's hair. Usually she enjoyed the feel of it—thick and silky. But now all she cared about was how it looked. She wanted every guy in the room to wish he was Alex. And every girl to know that's what every guy was wishing.

When the song ended, Isabel felt confident her mission had been accomplished. "I'm going outside for a minute," she told Alex. He nodded, and she pushed her way out to the backyard. She took in a couple of deep lungfuls of the crisp night air. Then she spotted Michael over by the willow tree.

Isabel wandered over. It was the first time they'd been alone together since Max had told them about the *akino*. She didn't really feel like talking about it right now.

Michael wrapped his arm around her shoulders, and she leaned into him. Mmmm, yeah, that was the feeling she was looking for. To feel his strong shoulders against her back and know that he understood what she was feeling. Because he was feeling it himself.

Maria spotted Alex sitting halfway up Corrine's steps. She made her way over and plopped down next to him on the shag carpet. She was surprised that Corrine—the most materialistic, superficial girl Maria'd ever met—tolerated shag carpet in her own house. Maybe she'd convinced herself it had cool retro appeal.

"Have you seen Isabel? She disappeared on me," Alex asked.

Seems to be a trend, she thought. But of course, Michael wasn't her boyfriend. She couldn't expect him to spend the party with her.

"Last time I saw her, she was dancing with you,"

Maria answered. "By the way, it was quite a show. Girls were, like, about to start shoving dollar bills down your pants."

"Cool," Alex answered, but he seemed a little distracted.

"There's something I want to ask you," Maria told him. "In your capacity as guy best friend whose job it is to explain the workings of the male mind."

"Uh, okay." He plucked a strand out of the shag carpet and rolled it between his fingers. "What color would you say this is?"

"Burnt umber," she answered quickly. "Now, if a girl tells a guy that she loves him, shouldn't he be obligated to give her some kind of response? In words, I mean."

"Wait, let me get out my copy of *Men Are from Mars, Women Are from Venus*," Alex joked, his eyes restlessly searching the crowd.

Maria was glad he was only half paying attention. If he was focusing on her the way he usually did when they talked, he'd have realized she was talking about herself, and he'd try to get all the gory details.

"I guess as your representative guy, I'd have to say that lack of words *is* a kind of response," Alex continued. "Maybe just not the response a girl wants to hear."

"So it means the guy doesn't feel the same way?" Maria pushed. She started chewing on the ends of her hair, then caught herself. Gross! She hadn't done that since she was about nine.

121

"Uhhh, well, it could," he answered. "But some guys are just not word guys. They could feel the I-love-you thing on the inside but not be able to actually spit it out."

"I just have to say that you've been no help to me," Maria informed him.

"Look, words are overrated," Alex said. "You know how someone feels about you by how they treat you. That's what it comes down to. Now I'm going to go find Isabel, the Vanishing Woman." He stood up and left Maria sitting on the steps alone.

How he treats me, she thought. How he treats me is that he's not getting close enough to treat me in any way at all.

Liz quietly opened her front door. She didn't know why she bothered to be quiet. Her parents always wanted her to tell them when she got home, whether they were sleeping or not.

She headed straight to their bedroom door and gave a quick double knock, followed by three slow ones. She called it the made-it-back-alive-and-drug-free knock. But only to herself, of course.

"Good night, *mi hija*," her papa called.

"Night," she answered. She wondered if she should phone over to Corrine's and tell Maria or somebody that she wasn't coming. No, they'd figure it out.

She wandered down the hall to the kitchen. She thought she'd get some milk, maybe even some turkey if there was any left. She knew it was going to be one of those nights when she needed a little help going to sleep.

Liz reached for the fridge handle and noticed that a new picture of her had appeared on the door. It was truly embarrassing to see her own face wallpapering the fridge.

At least when Rosa was alive, pictures of her had taken up half the space. Liz reminded herself that she had to go through the basement and see if she could find those pictures. Every single photo of Rosa had disappeared the day after she died.

Not that Liz needed them to remember her sister. She thought about her every day. The same way she'd think of Max.

If . . .

12

"I wish I could go out with you guys again tonight," Maria said from her perch on the edge of Alex's chair. "But my dad bought these concert tickets a long time ago. He's really psyched for father-daughter bonding—just me and him, no Kevin."

"Go and bond. It's fine," Max told her. "If anyone else has something to do, go ahead and do it. You've spent the whole day crawling across the desert floor around the chicken rock."

He almost wished they would all go away. At least for a while. It felt so strange being at the center of all this attention—all this anxious, watchful, careful attention.

Michael spread his map out on the Evanses' coffee table. They were using Max and Isabel's place as their home base because their parents were spending the weekend in Clovis, where they had their second office. They had so much work to get done for Monday that they figured it was a waste to drive all the way back to Roswell just to sleep.

"We'll just keep extending our search out in a widening circle around the rock," Michael explained. "Plus Ray's going to keep the area on

125

round-the-clock surveillance. He might be able to spot someone on their way into the compound and follow them."

Maria stood up and grabbed her backpack. Then she rushed over, practically flung herself at Max, and kissed him on the cheek, her aura swooshing through his. "Okay, I'm going. Bye." She turned around and rushed out of the room before he could react.

Max hoped he was wrong, but he thought he'd heard the sound of tears in her voice. If Maria was going to cry every time she looked at him, he really wouldn't be able to take it.

"Alex and Isabel, you take this section," Michael continued. "And Liz and Max—"

He was interrupted by Maria dashing back into the room. "I have an idea. It's kind of wacky, but it might work," she burst out. "You guys know how to use your power to change people's appearance, right?"

Max nodded. He'd only done it once, besides practicing with Ray. And that was to spy on Liz when she was out with another guy. Max glanced over at her, and she smiled at him. He knew she was thinking about the same thing.

"Anyway, I thought all of you could go out to different bars and stuff looking like the guard I *saw* at the compound where the ship is kept. His face is burned into my memory," Maria explained. "Then maybe somebody who knows the guard, the real guard, will come up and start a conversation. If it's somebody he knows from work—"

"We could get some key information," Michael interrupted. "I think it's definitely worth a shot." He turned to Max. "Want to try it?"

"Why not?" Max asked. Then he remembered. The *akino* had destroyed his power. How could he have forgotten that? "You and Isabel will have to do it for Liz and Alex and me," he admitted. "I can't do . . . anything like that anymore."

"Just tell us how," Isabel said quickly.

He hated feeling so helpless. What was next? Would someone have to spoon-feed him? Wipe his butt for him? What?

"It's not that much different from healing," he told Isabel and Michael. "Except instead of squeezing the molecules to close a cut or something, you squeeze them and push them to form the skin and bone into different shapes."

"I'll try it on Liz," Michael said.

Max got up and traded places with Michael so he could be next to Liz. He wasn't too happy with the idea of Michael connecting to Liz, touching her. But he knew he was being a big baby, and he told himself to just get over it.

Maria described the guard with enthusiastic hand movements. "All right, so he had roundish, middle-aged cheeks . . . and deep laugh lines . . . and a flat, wide nose."

Michael's eyes widened as he touched his fingertips to Liz's face. His hands began to massage her cheeks, kneading them like dough. He listened to Maria's suggestions and sculpted Liz's face accordingly. In no time

Liz's face looked like a middle-aged man's. Michael pulled back his hands and showed Maria the results.

"No, no, no. I'm sorry. It just doesn't look like the image in my head. What if I connect to you, Michael, and transmit my mental picture to you?" Maria asked.

"Let's try it," Michael said.

Maria connected to Michael. He placed his hands on Liz's face again, and it slowly began to morph—the eyes from blue to brown, bushier eyebrows, and a slight double chin. "That's it, that's it," Maria urged him on.

Michael's hands glided up into Liz's hair. It turned mottled orange, then lightened to dishwater blond, and finally changed to white, shrinking in length as it made the color switch. The final result was bristly, just longer than a crew cut.

"Perfect. It's like that doll," Maria mumbled. "You know the one where you could sort of reel its hair back into its head to make it short?"

Liz glanced over her shoulder at Max. "How do I look as a blond? A practically bald blond, I mean," she asked, running her fingers over her buzz cut.

"I wouldn't kick you out of bed," Michael answered before Max could.

"Come on. Let's get on with this," Isabel demanded. "I want to get out of here."

After a couple minutes' work Liz was ready. The Maria-Michael connection moved on to Alex. Isabel decided to morph herself.

"I'm going to get something to drink," Max said.

He felt so useless here. Maria giving instructions. Isabel and Michael working on Alex and Liz. And him sitting there twiddling his thumbs. The word *loser* came to mind.

He slowly made his way into the kitchen, his feet feeling as heavy as cement blocks. He dropped down into the closest chair and rested his head on the table. In here, alone, he didn't have to pretend that he wasn't absolutely exhausted, to the point where just sitting up and breathing felt like a workout.

"Max, your turn," Michael called. Max jerked up his head. How could they be done with Liz and Alex already? He checked the clock on the kitchen stove and realized he'd been sitting there for almost half an hour. He must have dozed off. Usually he couldn't sleep more than his two hours a night even if he wanted to. Now he was dropping off without even realizing it.

Max shoved himself to his feet, and a tremor sizzled through his legs. He took a deep breath and focused on making it into the living room and keeping the fear off his face. "I think I'm going to have to stay here," he admitted as he lowered himself to the couch.

"I'll stay with you," Liz immediately volunteered. At least he thought it was her. The words had come out of the mouth of a burly blond guy with a husky voice and a nondescript gray security guard's outfit. Michael obviously hadn't missed the vocal cords when he made the transformation.

"I don't need a baby-sitter," he answered, trying

to keep the irritation out of his tone. "Getting information on the ship, that's the most important thing you can do for me," he added, trying to reassure her.

She nodded and turned to the other two "guards." Isabel had already finished the job on Alex and done herself. "We should pick different parts of town," Liz told them. "Two of us can't show up at the same place." They began dividing up the town's bars and clubs as they headed out of the room.

"Be careful," Max called after them as they left for their mission. "Call if . . . you need something."

Like there was anything he'd be able to do if they did.

"You can be our Charlie, and we'll be your Angels," Alex called back. At least Max was pretty sure it was Alex. The voice was the same as Liz's, but it was an Alex kind of thing to say.

"You better catch up with them and get an assignment," Max told Michael. "Liz is right. It could be dangerous if anyone sees two of you together. I'm not sure if the Project Clean Slate agents know we can change our appearance. But if they do, and they see two guards—"

"I'm not going out," Michael interrupted.

"You're not staying with me," Max protested.

"So do you want to lie on the couch? Or do you want to go to bed?" Michael asked matter-of-factly.

Max gave up. "Bed, I guess."

Michael crossed over to him and reached out his hand. Max took it and let Michael help him to his feet.

* * *

Alex had a moment of anxiety when he walked into Moe's, one of the few places in Roswell that didn't have some kind of alien theme going on. Then he realized that there was no way he was going to get carded. He was, like, thirty years old or something.

He headed up to the bar and ordered a ginger ale. He figured the color could pass for a mixed drink, so he wouldn't feel like a total wuss.

Alex did a quick scan of the room. Whew, no Dad. He thought he might see his father there because Moe's was the hangout for the town's retired military guys. Alex didn't know if Project Clean Slate had any military connection, but it seemed likely that it could, so he figured Moe's was a decent place to find somebody who knew the guard.

He tossed aside the ridiculously thin straw and gulped down some of the ginger ale while he took a slower look around. He was hoping someone would give him a nod, or a half wave, anything that showed they had seen him—the guard—before. No dice.

If the guard came in here often enough, the bartender would probably recognize him. But the place was packed, so the guy had just slammed Alex's drink down and raced toward the end of the bar. So Alex couldn't get a sense of whether he recognized the guard or not.

When I get a second round, maybe I'll pretend like I have amnesia and ask him if he knows who I am. Alex snorted. He could just picture himself reeling around the bar with his hands pressed to his temples, murmuring, "Where am I? Who are you? Who am I?"

Maybe it would have been better to keep searching the area around the rock. But they could go back to that tomorrow. Alex couldn't help wondering how much time they had left.

Max was looking bad. The effects of the *akino* were speeding up. And it was really affecting his body now. In less than a day his face had thinned out. You could practically see the bones pushing their way through his thin, translucent skin. Alex felt a pang of shock every time he looked at Max.

"Scotch. Rocks," a voice ordered behind him.

A way too familiar voice. You knew it could happen, Alex reminded himself. He glanced over and saw his dad sliding onto the next bar stool.

"You military?" he asked Alex.

Of course. His dad grouped everyone into military or not military. He'd want to know who he was dealing with.

"Navy," Alex answered. It just sprang from his mouth, maybe because Jesse had been talking about it so much. Maybe because, for once, he had an opportunity to impress his dad.

"Have one in the navy, one in the marines," his dad answered.

Obviously I'm not worth mentioning, Alex thought. "Any other kids?" he asked, just to see if his dad would continue to deny Alex's existence under direct questioning.

"One. Senior in high school and he has no idea

what he wants to do with his life. None," his dad answered.

"Huh," Alex grunted. Then he realized he had a real opportunity. A chance to bait Pops for his own benefit.

"Sounds like my brother, Willy," Alex commented. "My dad was really worried about him. He tried to straighten him out by getting him to start an ROTC program at his high school. But Willy . . . he kept weaseling out of it. Too busy farting around on his computer and chasing after girls to bother. He managed to graduate without accomplishing a damn thing." That last bit was pretty much a direct quote from his dad about what was going to happen to Alex.

"Exactly." His dad pounded his fist on the bar. "Exactly like my son. He doesn't realize that what he does in the next couple of years will determine the course of his entire life."

You suck down that bait, Dad, Alex thought, starting to really enjoy his little fishing trip.

"So how'd this brother of yours turn out?" Alex's dad asked.

"You aren't going to believe this," Alex answered. He drained his ginger ale, savoring the moment before he reeled his dad in and left him gasping on the shore.

"Willy's done real well for himself. You've probably heard of him. He goes by Bill now. Bill Gates."

His dad choked on an ice cube.

Alex grinned. Yeah, Dad. Think of that next time

you start harassing me about the ROTC. I could grow up to be a big software designer who owns pretty much half the known universe.

Isabel pulled the Jeep into the Weather Balloon's parking lot. The neon sign cast a rainbow of colors over the asphalt—the blue of the balloon, the green of the little alien who kept peeking out from behind it, the red of the alien's ray gun.

She hopped out of the Jeep and stumbled. She was still getting used to her new body. The guard had some serious mass, most of it muscle, but still.

A fortyish woman in leggings with little green men all over them smiled at Isabel as she approached the door. Isabel smiled back. She believed in being kind to the less fortunate. And anyone who thought she was attractive enough to wear those leggings in public definitely qualified.

The woman's smile grew even wider. Flirtatious.

Isabel gave a soft little groan. She thinks I'm coming on to her, Isabel realized. She thinks I'm a bleached-blond male bimbo—a, uh, mimbo ripe for the picking.

She made a blank facial expression as she walked past the woman and into the bar. Yeah, she was a guy, but unwanted attention was unwanted attention. And Isabel knew how to deal with that.

Oh no. Wait, she thought. What if that woman knew me—the guard? What if I just blew off the person I came here hoping to find?

Isabel glanced at the woman. She wasn't shooting

any evil glances in the guard's direction, which she probably would have had she known him and he just walked right by her like that.

This acting-like-the-guard assignment was going to be trickier than she'd thought. She spotted an empty table and headed over. Then she sat down and crossed her legs.

Very masculine, she scolded herself. She uncrossed her legs and did that thing guys do, where they take up as much space as they possibly can. She draped her arm over the rail next to the table and spread her legs wide apart. Yeah, she was a man. Give her some room.

Max would crack up if he could see her right now. His little sister working the big strongman thing.

The thought of Max sent a stab of fear through her. The *akino* seemed to be entering a new stage— attacking his body. And what was she doing to help him? Sitting in a bar trying to remember not to cross her legs like a girl.

A waitress in a tight Weather Balloons T-shirt hurried up to her table. The double *O*s in *Balloon* were extra big—and positioned right over her chest. Poor girl, Isabel thought. She must get a lot of comments from the classy guys who hang out here.

"I'll have a beer," Isabel said, making sure to look the waitress right in the eye. She figured she was probably the only guy not to stare at her *O*s all night. The waitress must have appreciated it, too, because she was back with Isabel's drink within seconds.

Isabel pretended to take a swallow of beer. She'd only ordered it because it seemed like what a guy like her would order. Besides, if she'd ordered a soda, she would have been tempted to drink it, and then she might have to pee, and peeing was not something she wanted to attempt in this body.

I wish I knew what my name is supposed to be, she thought. Someone could be calling me from the other side of the room and I wouldn't know it. She did a check of the crowd, moving her eyes quickly from person to person, careful not to give any of the ladies any ideas.

Her eyes lingered on the clock behind the bar. It had been almost an hour since she'd seen Max. She was almost afraid to go home when she was done here. Afraid to see what new changes she'd see in him.

Isabel scanned the crowd again, just in case she'd missed anyone. She didn't see even a flash of recognition on anyone's face. Maria's plan was insane. This was never going to work. And searching for the compound was turning out to be one step above counting all the grains of sand in the desert. Just another flavor of impossible.

A squeal from the next table jerked her attention in that direction. Her waitress was glaring at a prepster college boy and his two smirking buddies. The front of her T-shirt was soaked.

"Hey, sorry," prepster boy said, not very sincerely. "I thought I heard them announce the start of the wet T-shirt contest. You wanted to enter, right?"

"Wrong," Isabel answered for her. This was one problem that wasn't impossible, and it would be her very definite pleasure to deal with it. She turned to the prepster. "Apologize."

The prepster stared at her a moment, eyes glazed. Then he turned to the waitress.

"I'm sorry," he told the waitress. Then he winked at his buds. "Let me help dry you off."

Isabel leaped up before he could touch the girl. She grabbed him by the front of his shirt and yanked him out from behind his table. Then she pulled back her meaty arm and slammed her fist into his nose. She smiled when it squirted blood.

It was good to have a problem with an easy solution.

Liz felt someone tap her on the shoulder. This was great. She'd only been at UFOnics for about half an hour, and somebody had recognized her. She turned around and felt a jolt of pure dread.

Sheriff Valenti stood in front of her. "Come with me," he ordered. He turned around and headed for the exit.

He thinks you're the guard, she told herself as she followed him out into the parking lot. He thinks you're some guy who works at the compound. This could be a chance to get some good info. Just chill.

Valenti headed straight for his cruiser. The sound of his boot heels against the pavement made her teeth ache. He climbed into the car, obviously assuming she'd just get in, too, without asking for any more information.

Liz walked around to the passenger door, hoping she didn't move too differently from the guard. She didn't have an especially girlie walk in her own body, so she was probably doing okay. She jerked open the door, slid inside, and slammed it closed.

She took a fast peek at Valenti. For once he wasn't wearing his mirrored shades. But it was still impossible to figure out what he was thinking. If Valenti's eyes were the mirror to his soul, then clearly he didn't have one. Alert the media. As if that wasn't painfully obvious already.

Valenti pulled out of the parking lot and headed away from the center of town. "You need to take part in some tests at the compound. Nerz got sick, and no one but you has clearance. Fortunately you're predictable in your after-hours activities."

Liz felt relief explode through her like a fireworks show. Maybe once she got inside the compound, she'd be able to find a way on board the ship. Maybe she'd be able to get the crystals tonight! Even if she didn't, they would be so much closer to saving Max's life than they had been before.

"Something amusing you, Towner?" Valenti asked. Probably because her smile was covering her entire face.

Now at least she knew her name. Towner. "No. Just thinking of a joke someone told me," Liz answered. She figured there was no chance Valenti would be interested enough in humor to ask, and she was right.

As they passed the chamber of commerce billboard on the outskirts of town, Liz checked the odometer. When they pulled off the highway, she'd check it again. She could hardly believe she was being handed the location of the compound by Sheriff Valenti himself.

Unless . . . what if the real guard is already at the compound? she thought. What if Valenti knows

140

that? What if that's why he's bringing me there—because he thinks I'm an alien with the ability to alter my appearance? What if he doesn't care if I know the location because he's not planning on ever letting me leave?

Suddenly it felt as if half the air had been sucked out of the cruiser. And the air that remained was thick with the odor of smoke and sweat.

Even if all that's true, there's nothing you can do about it now, she told herself. What, are you going to dive out of a moving car and take off into the desert? Valenti would probably shoot you.

That thought didn't help her anxiety. She stared out at the empty highway and tried to count the dotted lines as they sped by. She needed something to focus on. But Valenti was going too fast.

He made a sharp left and swung the cruiser off into the desert. He was heading toward the chicken rock. At least Maria got that part right.

Two-and-a-third miles later, they passed the rock. The cruiser kept bouncing across the desert in a straight line.

Liz's eyes kept darting to the odometer. Three miles. Seven. Eleven. Fourteen. They were heading toward a large rock formation. That would be a good landmark. She'd have to remember it.

"Open the entrance," Valenti told her.

Liz's heart lurched up to her throat. Obviously this was something she was supposed to know how to do. There must be some kind of remote or something. She hoped.

She popped open the glove compartment. Papers. Sunglasses. A couple of flares.

"Exactly how much did you have to drink tonight?" Valenti asked.

"I didn't know I'd be working," Liz answered.

Valenti gave a disgusted snort. Then he grabbed what looked like an ordinary garage door opener with a few extra buttons off the dashboard and thrust it at her.

Pick a button, any button, Liz thought wildly. She jammed down the one closest to her thumb. Nothing happened. She shot a glance at Valenti. Had he noticed?

Don't think about that, just try another one, she ordered herself. She stabbed down the button in the upper-left corner. Nothing. She tried the one next to it . . . and the middle of the rock formation split open.

No wonder Max and Michael searched for years without finding this place, she thought. A gasp escaped from her lips. She tried to cover it with a coughing fit. Was Valenti picking up on any of her little screwups? There was no way to tell. His face was impassive, as always. She bet he didn't even blink when he shot Nikolas.

Don't go there, she thought. She couldn't think about Valenti killing someone. She was way too nervous already.

Liz struggled to keep any sign of amazement off her face as Valenti drove straight into the opening. I'm probably supposed to shut the door, too, she thought. She hit the button that had worked the last time. With astonishing speed the doors slammed shut. Clipping off one of Valenti's tail-lights.

"Sorry," she mumbled.

"No problem. I'll take it out of your salary," he answered.

Sorry to you, too, Towner, Liz thought as the car started to descend with a slow, even motion.

They'd driven into a massive elevator. It opened into an underground parking garage. Valenti pulled into a space marked Reserved.

He climbed out of the car, again assuming Liz would follow. She scrambled after him. He led the way down a long cement corridor, like the one Maria had seen the night she used the Stone to track him.

Liz was so close. The ship could be around any corner.

They reached a huge metal door. Valenti keyed in a code. The door split open, and they continued into a huge open room. Inside were two rows of glass cells. There was a bed in each of them, but only one was made up.

A shudder swept through Liz. Is this where Max, Michael, and Isabel would be brought if Valenti ever learned the truth about them? Would they be kept in here like lab animals, constantly monitored?

Valenti crossed the room without speaking to either of the guards stationed near the cell that seemed to have been recently occupied. He unlocked a smaller door and held it open for Liz.

"You'll be given your instructions in a moment," he informed her. The moment she stepped inside, he shut the door behind her and locked it.

The room was empty except for a metal table and one folding chair. Liz sat down and waited. At least she was going to be given instructions. That was good. No one was expecting her to already know what she was doing.

"Towner, all you are doing tonight is describing anything that occurs in your room," a voice said through the intercom.

Liz shifted her weight on the cold metal chair. Anything that occurs in your room. She didn't quite like the sound of that. What were these experiments, anyway? They had to connect to aliens somehow, didn't they? Or was that only one area Project Clean Slate covered?

What if these tests were to determine the effect of some new biological weapon? Some smart virus or something?

It was too late to worry about that now. She was pretty sure the door was locked from the outside. And even if it wasn't, she—

Wait. Something was happening. Liz cleared her throat. "Um, I see a spot of shimmering air at about eye level. It's approximately the size of a basketball."

Liz gripped the edge of the table with both hands, waiting to see what would happen next. A moment later an image formed in the circle.

"I see an image that looks like a hologram. It's a man sitting in a restaurant. Fancy. White tablecloth.

144

Candles. I can hear violin music. And I can tell the man is excited. Nervous. Happy. All of those."

Liz didn't know how, but she was getting *feelings* from the man in the hologram. It's like what Max described when he told me how Ray showed him a hologram of his parents' ship crashing, she realized.

So maybe that was what was going on. Maybe the Project Clean Slate agents were trying to duplicate alien technology or something. She relaxed her grip on the table. She was going to get through this okay. All she had to do was look at some floating pictures. And if she was lucky, she'd get a glimpse of the ship on her way out.

"Anything else?" the voice asked through the intercom.

Liz studied the hologram. "I know he's getting ready to ask his girlfriend to marry him," she said. "I don't know how I know. It's not like I can hear his thoughts or anything. But I just . . . know."

The hologram disappeared. Bummer. I didn't even get to find out what she said, Liz thought. She was feeling a little giddy. Or woozy, like she'd had way too much cough medicine . . . while bouncing on a trampoline.

The air in front of her began to shimmer again. Oh, goody. Time for the second feature. Liz wondered how they—whoever they were—would feel about a request for popcorn with lots of that fake butter flavoring.

"Oh, I forgot to say the air has started to shimmer," she said quickly. She didn't want to get

Towner in any more trouble than he already was.

"The hologram has appeared," she continued. "It's another restaurant. I've seen it in town. The Crashdown Café. There are two men sitting in a booth."

Liz's heart slammed up her throat when she recognized them. The day she got shot. Oh God, the day she got shot, these two were in the café. Fighting. The muscular man, he was the one who'd pulled the gun. He aimed for the beefy guy, but the beefy guy knocked his arm away. The gun went off, and the next thing Liz knew she was slammed against the wall, her stomach wet with her own blood.

"Go on," the voice said over the intercom.

"The men are both angry. They each think the other one cheated them out of some money," Liz said, trying to sound like this meant nothing to her.

This time the hologram let her see what happened next. She got to see the gun drawn again. See the shot fired.

"The more muscular man just shot a waitress. I can feel the pain from her," Liz continued.

And she could. She could feel the pain again. Exactly as she'd felt it that day.

Exactly.

Oh God. Somehow they were getting the image from her. This time the hologram was like a memory playback. Like when Ray showed Max the ship. That must be why she'd been feeling so weird and dizzy. Someone had been accessing her brain.

And in about two more seconds the hologram projector would show Max vault over the counter and heal Liz's gunshot wound with the touch of his hands.

Liz let out a piercing scream. "Make it stop," she howled. "It's like a drill going through my eyeballs. Make it stop."

The hologram disappeared. Valenti burst through the door.

Liz pressed the heels of her hands against her eyes and doubled over. Was Valenti buying this? Did he believe she was in agony? Or had he discovered her disguise and decided to torture her?

Slowly Liz lowered her hands.

"What the hell happened?" Valenti demanded.

"You tell me," Liz shot back. "I felt like my head was going to explode. I didn't sign up for this."

"I'll get you an escort home," Valenti answered. "But I better not find out that your exploding head was alcohol induced."

He gave her a long look as she walked past him. Clearly he had the feeling something was off, but he couldn't figure out exactly what.

Liz wondered if he'd make the connection when they came back in and stole the crystals.

14

Maria felt tears burn her eyes—again. *Aren't you just a little ray of sunshine?* she asked herself. In another minute Max was going to ban her from his room permanently. She could tell that her crying made him really uncomfortable.

And why wouldn't it? It was like she was holding up a big sign that said, "Guess what, Max? You're dying!"

He looked *bad,* though. All sunken in on himself. The others had noticed it, too. Liz, Isabel, and Michael kept taking cautious little glances at him. They were careful not to stare but were obviously shaken by his appearance.

When Alex burst into the room, she was very happy for the distraction. "Sorry I'm late," he told them. "My dad wouldn't let me leave the house until I showed him my web page, if you can believe that."

"We're trying to figure out the best way into the compound. Any ideas?" Michael asked him.

The doorbell rang before he could answer. "I got it," Maria said. She rushed out. On the way to the door she pulled a vial of cedar oil out of her pocket and took a few deep breaths. It hadn't been helping her much lately, but it was better than nothing.

She swung open the door and found Ray Iburg standing there. "We're all in Max's room," she told him as she led the way back.

"I thought you might need an extra power source when you go into the compound," he said as they stepped through the doorway.

"Great. We might need a shield like the one that froze Valenti in the mall," Michael answered.

Ray shook his head. "I'm not recharged enough for that yet. It took a huge amount of power. I won't be able to do it again for probably a month," he explained. "But I can still knock someone out if I have to."

"That could also be useful," Michael said. "Okay, the team will be you, me, and Isabel, then."

He was in commando mode. Focused entirely on strategy. For once Maria didn't have to wonder if he was thinking about Isabel or her. He wasn't thinking about either of them.

"Wait. I—," Alex began to protest.

"You don't have powers to protect yourself," Michael cut him off.

Alex nodded. It made sense to Maria, too. And it reminded her for about the millionth time that Michael and Isabel were close in a way that she and Michael could never be. Michael and Isabel shared the same powers, the same history. Michael and Maria shared the same taste in movies. Huh. Now, class, which is the basis for a real relationship?

"Why doesn't one of you change your appearance

to look like Valenti?" Liz asked, rapid-fire fast. "Valenti rules that place. As him, you'd have access to everything."

"Perfect plan. I'll do it," Michael said.

"You and I should change our appearance, too," Ray told Isabel. "That way when they come looking for us, we can just disappear."

"We need to make sure that Valenti's not already at the compound before you head out. I'll call his house. Say I want them to switch their long-distance carrier or something." Alex hurried out of the room.

Max pulled in a long, rasping, rattling breath. A breath that sounded so painful, Maria didn't know how he could stand to keep breathing.

What if they don't get back in time? That was the thought she'd been trying to keep from thinking. She raked her fingers through her hair and tried to bury the thought again.

Alex rushed back into the room. "He's there. And he was not happy to get a sales call on a Sunday morning."

"You should go stake out his house," Michael said.

"I'll go, too," Maria volunteered. She couldn't stay here with Max—her aura was too filled with grief already.

"What are you going to do if he leaves for the compound?" Liz asked. "You don't have any way to warn Michael."

"I'll stop him," Alex answered, with total conviction.

Maria believed him. Alex had more than a little commando in him, too, much as he didn't want to be Mr. Military.

"Let's go," Alex told Maria.

She obediently moved toward the door. But then she turned and looked back into the room. Her eyes sought out Michael. This could be the last time she ever saw him.

Liz stared down at Max's face. He'd fallen into a restless sleep, so for once she could really look at him, study the changes in him, without worrying that she would frighten him.

She noted each detail as if she were in bio lab. Somehow that made it a little easier. Small patches of his skin were flaking away. His lips were dry and chapped, with a few spots of dried blood. His eyes were sunk deep into his head. His cheeks were sunken, too. His neck was—

Stop, she thought. Stop reducing him to all these little pieces of damaged flesh. This is Max. It's still Max, the guy you love.

Liz reached out and took his hand. She wondered if the sensation worked its way into his dreams somehow. She hoped so.

She checked her watch. Michael, Isabel, and Ray should be at the compound soon. She wondered how long it would take them to find the crystals. She was afraid that—even if they found them immediately—it would be too late. Max's deterioration was accelerating at a terrifying rate.

He was slipping away from her, and she was powerless to stop him. She tightened her grip on his hand, lacing her fingers with his. But it wasn't enough. She needed to be closer to him. Even closer.

Liz kicked off her shoes and climbed into bed next to Max. She wrapped her arm across his chest and buried her face in his shoulder. "I'm not going to let you go, Max," she whispered.

He was so cold. It was like his body wasn't throwing off any heat at all. She pressed herself closer, trying to share her warmth with him. "I love you, Max," she said. "I love you. Stay with me, okay? You've got to stay with me."

She pulled Max's arm around her, trying to get closer still. It lay there limp and heavy. Lifeless. The arm of a corpse.

She sat up fast and sprang off the bed. She pressed her fingers against Max's lips and felt the reassuring puff of air as he let out a breath. "Sorry, Max," she whispered. "I didn't mean to freak." She smoothed the covers over him and fluffed his pillow. She felt something hard and cool against her fingers and pulled it out.

Her silver bracelet. Max had turned it to liquid on her wrist the day that he had told her he was an alien. He had been trying to convince her he wasn't lying.

She'd been so totally terrified. Terrified of Max. When he'd re-formed the bracelet and taken a step toward her to give it to her, she'd bolted.

And he'd kept it. He'd actually been sleeping with it under his pillow. Liz ran her finger over the braided silver, and the tears came flooding out of

153

her. Max didn't need this seeping into his dreams. He didn't need her weak and wailing. He needed her to be strong, holding on tight, willing him to live.

She rushed out of his room and down the hall to the bathroom. She locked the door behind her and sat down on the edge of the tub, rocking back and forth, letting the sobs overtake her.

After a few minutes she stood up and moved to the sink. She splashed some cold water on her face and dried her face roughly. She met her gaze in the medicine cabinet mirror. "Enough," she said firmly. "Max needs you with him."

She turned and walked out of the bathroom and down the hall. When she stepped through Max's doorway, his eyes were open. He cleared his throat hard. "Was I dreaming . . ." He cleared his throat again. "Or were you in bed with me before?" he asked.

She smiled at him. "You weren't dreaming," she answered.

"Not how . . . I imagined it."

It was obvious the words were taking a tremendous effort. Droplets of sweat were running down his face. He winced as they stung the cracks in his skin.

"There will be another time," she promised him.

She hoped she was telling the truth.

"Liz said there was some kind of remote to open a door in the rock formation, which we don't have," Michael said as they drove the car Ray had rented toward the compound.

Michael hadn't even thought about the fact that the Project Clean Slate people could trace a car as easily as they could a face. Easier. He was glad Ray had had the idea of renting the car under one of his old identities. Ray had switched faces and names a few times since he'd been stranded on earth.

"I'm sure they have some kind of surveillance cameras," Ray answered. "We'll just give them a good look at your Valenti mug, and I'm sure someone will scurry right out and let us in. Probably even apologize for not doing it faster."

That worked for Michael. There were advantages to being a Valenti clone. Although every time he caught sight of his gray eyes in the rearview mirror, it gave him the wiggins.

Michael's own eyes were gray, so it wasn't that much of a color change. But he couldn't shake the feeling that when he looked into his reflection, it was Valenti staring back. Valenti, the guy who wanted him dead or locked up in one of those cells Liz had seen and experimented on for the rest of his life.

"You okay back there, Iz?" he asked over his shoulder.

"Yeah," she muttered.

Didn't sound convincing. He knew it was freaking her out to be in the same car with him looking like this. Isabel had had nightmares about Valenti from the time she was a little girl. The sheriff was the embodiment of her darkest fears about what could happen to her if anyone found out the truth.

"You're not going to ask if I'm okay?" Ray joked.

"You better be because we've arrived," Michael answered. He pulled to a stop in front of the rock formation. Michael got out of the car and stared straight ahead, trying to look mildly pissed off. A moment later a massive door slid open.

"Welcome to the Bat Cave," Michael muttered as he slid back behind the wheel. He pulled into the elevator Liz had told them about, and when they got to the bottom, he parked in the reserved space. He was Valenti. The big cheeseball.

A guard hustled over as soon as he, Ray, and Isabel set foot out of the car. "We weren't expecting you until tonight," he said.

"That's why I'm here. I want to see what things are like when I'm not expected," Michael answered. He didn't bother to tell him who Ray and Isabel were. He figured Valenti wouldn't bother to explain himself to a peon.

Liz's plan was working out great. He could just

act like he was doing some kind of inspection or even giving Ray and Isabel a tour, and they could search every inch of the place.

But actually, why search? This peon would fall all over himself to do whatever Valenti wanted. "I want to show my associates the ship," he said.

My associates. He liked that. Kind of mysterious and you're-way-too-insignificant-to-know-who-they-really-are. Maybe he should take this show on the road. Do a tour as a Valenti impersonator.

He couldn't believe that thought had popped into his mind. He felt like he was partially buzzed or something. He was actually going to see the ship. He'd spent almost his whole life looking for it, and it was here.

The guard nodded and led the way through a maze of cement corridors, stopping now and then to punch in a security code. When they reached a huge set of metal doors, the guard stepped back. He obviously wanted Michael to do something, but what?

"Please step up to the red line and remove glasses for retina scan," an automated female voice instructed.

Michael automatically moved into position, but his intestines were practically squirming around inside him. His eyes looked like Valenti's, sure. But there's no way his retinas would be a match. No possible way.

A beam of light passed over his eyes.

"Individual not identified," the voice announced. "Access denied."

The guard pulled out a walkie-talkie and mumbled

157

into it. This was it. They were toast. Unless they moved pretty damn fast.

Ray moved up behind the guard, ready to knock him out. Isabel looked ready to take on everyone in the whole place, judging from her narrowed eyes and the way her hands had curled into fists at her sides. Time to rock and roll, Michael thought. Then the doors slid open.

"I'll get someone to go over the system," the guard said, his face pink with embarrassment.

Was it really going to be this easy? Not that he was complaining.

"You do that," Michael answered as he stepped through the doors, Ray and Isabel close beside him.

The ship lay before them. A sleek wedge of metal that was smaller than Michael expected. But looking at it, he found it hard to breathe.

This ship had been built on a planet in a galaxy that humans didn't even have a name for. It had carried his parents all the way here. And they had died inside it when they began the return voyage.

Michael felt like he could stand here for hours, just staring at it. The construction was awesome. He didn't see a seam. Not a bolt. Not a rivet. Nothing. Talk about aerodynamic. The metal itself was even more mind-bending. In places it looked almost liquid. Molten. Rippling as if alive.

Isabel elbowed him. "We have a timetable to keep, Sheriff," she said.

"Right." Michael strode over to the ship, then

hesitated. Where were the doors on this thing? He didn't see a handle.

Ray reached out and touched a small raised circle, and a door appeared. Isabel took a deep breath and stepped across the threshold.

"Go ahead," Ray told Michael.

Michael started inside. He'd pretty much given up the hope that this day would ever come. But he was standing on board the ship. He reached out and lightly ran his fingers across the closest wall.

Then he crumpled to his knees, pain clawing through him. Pain from Max, stronger than anything he'd ever felt.

"Sheriff Valenti, are you all right?" a guard shouted.

Footsteps rushed toward him as another slash of pain hit. He felt his face . . . moving. Twisting. He couldn't hold on to the changes he'd made in his molecular structure.

A guard grabbed Michael by the shoulder—and saw his face. *His* face. Not Valenti's.

"Something's up," Alex told Maria.

Valenti had just burst out of his house. He strode over to his cruiser, his face set and grim. This was not a man on his way to the grocery store.

"What are we going to do?" Maria demanded, her voice high and shrill.

"Follow him," Alex answered.

Maybe he found out that his girlfriend was cheating on him, Alex thought as he waited for the cruiser to pass their stakeout spot. Or that Kyle had been busted for smoking a joint behind the school.

Not likely. It would be a pretty big coincidence for either of those things to happen right during the few hours when Michael, Isabel, and Ray were breaking into the compound.

"Go!" Maria cried. "You're going to lose him."

"Let me do this," Alex snapped. "I don't want him to notice us." He waited a few more seconds to let another car get between him and Valenti, then pulled out onto the street.

Valenti headed straight to the main road out of town. And yeah, he passed the grocery store.

"He's heading out of town! He's going to the compound! You said you would stop him! Why aren't you stopping him?" Maria shouted.

"I want to wait until we get a little ways into the desert," Alex answered. "It's too dangerous in town. I don't want to accidentally cream someone."

"Okay, okay. Okay, sorry," she said. "I didn't mean to yell. I just—"

"I know," Alex answered. "Me too."

Alex kept his eyes locked on Valenti as they reached the edge of town. Not that he had any doubt where Valenti was heading.

"Okay, I'm going to pull up next to him. You yell . . . something. That there's been a robbery or whatever. Any sheriff thing you can think of. Maybe that will be enough to make him turn back. Project Clean Slate *is* a secret. Valenti has to give at least an impersonation of a regular sheriff."

Maria nodded. "Ready when you are."

160

Alex hit the gas and pulled up even with Valenti. Maria leaned out the window. "The 7-Eleven was robbed," she yelled. "The owner was shot. You have to get back there."

Maria ducked back inside. "He didn't even turn his head. He had to see me, don't you think?"

"Yeah," Alex answered. "Time for plan B."

"Which is?" Maria demanded.

"I don't know exactly. But you better roll up the window and buckle your seat belt just in case," he told her.

As soon as Maria was strapped in, Alex jerked the wheel to the right. Metal screamed against metal as his Rabbit gave the cruiser a hard shove.

They definitely had Valenti's attention now. And he wasn't happy. He gave the Rabbit a sideways slam that sent it into a half turn across the lane.

Alex expected Valenti to take the opportunity to put some distance between their cars. But that wasn't his style. With a squeal of tires he jerked his cruiser around so that it was aimed at the Rabbit.

"Hold on, he's going to ram us!" Alex warned Maria.

A second later the cruiser bulldozed into the back of the Rabbit, slamming it out onto the desert. Valenti backed up, preparing for another slam. Alex saw him doing it. But he couldn't get out of the way in time. And there was no chance he could somehow circle to the side of Valenti and start ramming him.

Alex braced himself against the wheel as the cruiser took its second shot.

"The arroyo! He's pushing us toward the arroyo!" Maria cried as Valenti backed up again.

The narrow canyon wasn't that deep. But it wasn't going to be a fun landing. And once they were down there, there was no way they'd be able to stop Valenti.

Alex spat out a curse as he jerked the wheel to the left and floored the gas. Too late. The cruiser smashed into them again.

And the Rabbit sailed over the edge of the arroyo.

The pain sweeping through Isabel subsided. What did that mean? Now that she couldn't feel pain from Max, did that mean . . . did that mean he was dead?

Get the crystals, she told herself. That's all you can think about right now. She rushed down the ship's narrow walkway, her feet making a grating sound on the metal mesh of the floor.

Ray said the crystals were kept in one of the slots under the control panel. But where was the control panel? And where were Ray and Michael?

She couldn't risk going back to look for them. If she was the only one who'd made it onto the ship, she was Max's only hope.

She wished she had a map of the ship's interior. It was a lot bigger than she thought it was. It was as if the ship was larger inside than out, the walkways branching off in all directions. She wasn't sure she was even on the right one. She could be rushing completely the wrong way. She'd only picked this walkway because it looked slightly wider than the others.

Isabel's walkway widened and widened until it formed a large room with huge windows. She couldn't see anything out of them. She didn't know if it was some kind of cloaking mechanism or what. And she didn't care. She didn't see any controls of any kind, so she was obviously in the wrong place.

Two more walkways branched off the observation room. They looked pretty much identical. Isabel chose the closest one. She ran down it with her head ducked. It got wider and wider until it opened into a room that had something Isabel figured could be a control panel. Thank God.

Now where were those slots Ray mentioned? She didn't see anything that could be called a slot or a hole or a cubby or anything. She dashed over and slid her fingers over the smooth metal beneath the controls. She felt a little raised spot and hit it. A slot opened up. No crystals.

Isabel heard footsteps approaching. "Finally," she called. "I can use some help in here." She felt for another raised spot, then jammed it so hard, she broke a nail.

She started searching for another spot. Then she realized the footsteps were getting closer, but no one had answered her. Isabel felt the hairs at the back of her neck stand up. That meant that whoever was moving toward her wasn't Ray or Michael.

Oh, that was very smart, just announcing your exact location, Isabel thought. She slid both hands over the metal, searching for the next trigger. Found one. Hit it. No crystals.

The footsteps were very close now. Isabel swept her hands back and forth, leaving smears of sweat behind. She found another trigger spot. Punched it. And saw three crystals glowing softly in the dim light. She snatched them up and jammed them in her pockets.

"Hold it right there. Put your hands over your head," a voice commanded.

Isabel put her hands up and slowly turned. A guard stood blocking the center walkway. A guard with a machine gun over his chest.

Her eyes darted to the other two walkways. Could she make it to one of them in time? Or was that just a good way to get herself shot in the back?

"Get over here. And don't lower your hands, or I *will* shoot you," the guard ordered.

Isabel walked toward him. She was going to have to knock him out, and that meant touching him so she could make a connection.

She wondered how fast his reflexes were. Could he realize he was in danger and pull the trigger faster than she could find a nice vein in his head and squeeze?

At least she had her fake face back in place. Even better, the face was pretty. Not quite as pretty as her own, but still plenty pretty. That gave her a little advantage. Guys didn't tend to think of pretty girls as potentially lethal. Plus it made for a good distraction.

A couple more steps and she'd be close enough to reach him. Isabel made her bottom lip tremble a little, a trick she'd learned in the fourth grade. She hoped he'd think she was completely scared and helpless.

Isabel took a step, then another. Okay, hope this works, she thought. Because if it doesn't, one of us is leaving the compound in a body bag.

She took one more step, then pretended to stumble. She let herself fall, arms outstretched. The guard instinctively moved to catch her. His hand touched hers, and she willed herself to make the connection.

The rush of images began. Isabel let them rush past her in a blur of color. She heard the guard's heart begin to beat along with her own. Quickly she began to explore his body. *Their* body.

She chose a vein deep in his head and used her mind to *squeeze* the molecules together. She felt his pain and bewilderment, but she didn't let go. Not until he fell to the floor.

Isabel leaped over him and ran down the walkway to the observation room. She picked the widest walkway that branched off the room and sprinted down it.

She came to an abrupt halt when she reached the exit door. She could hear a fight going on. She took a step closer and leaned partway out. Her heart stopped, then gave a hard double slam in her chest.

Michael and Ray were battling against five guards. The guards had some kind of electrical stunners, like cattle prods. They were using them to keep Michael and Ray from touching them. There was one guard lying motionless on the ground. The others probably saw that Michael and Ray could hurt with a touch and were making very sure that neither of them got close enough to do any damage.

She hesitated, bouncing her weight from one foot to the other. Should she just make a run for it? That was probably her best chance of escaping. If she tried to help Michael and Ray, she might not get to Max in time. And Michael and Ray had each other for backup.

Yeah, she decided. She'd have to go without them. Isabel locked her eyes on the big metal doors leading out of the room. Then she ran full out.

She didn't know if the guards even saw her fly by. If they had, they weren't chasing her. Not yet. She wheeled around a corner and froze.

Sheriff Valenti was halfway down the cement hall, gun drawn. His cold gray eyes locked on her.

This was the moment Isabel had been fearing all her life. The moment the wolf came and dragged her off to his cave. One thing was clear—she would not let him take her alive.

"I don't want to shoot you. So be sensible. Don't try anything silly," Valenti said.

Of course he didn't want to shoot her. She was much more valuable to him alive. But the only way she was going to let him have her was dead.

Don't be insane, a little voice in her head

pleaded. Let him take you. Michael and Ray will come after you. You know that. There's no way Michael would let Valenti keep you here.

But Michael could die. Ray could die. And Isabel would be left at Valenti's mercy.

That thought decided her. Isabel let out a roar of rage and terror and launched herself at Valenti.

"Stop," he shouted. "Now!"

"Stop!" another voice yelled. A hand reached out and grabbed her by the back of the shirt. Isabel jerked her head to face her captor. Ray.

"Don't shoot. We're stopping. We're stopping right here," Ray told Valenti.

Ray was going to let Valenti take her. Examine her. Experiment on her. And finally dissect her.

No! Isabel jerked away and leaped toward the sheriff.

Ray flung himself in front of her. A shot rang out. And Ray fell to the ground, the green and blue whorls of his aura instantly turning black.

Oh God. Oh no. Ray was dead.

Isabel didn't want to leave him. Didn't want Valenti to have his poor, defenseless body. But Ray was dead. And Max was still alive.

She didn't hesitate more than a quarter of a second. She raced past Valenti and hurled herself around the next corner. She spotted another set of the metal doors. She dashed through them, then used her power to shove the molecules together, slamming the doors shut.

That's not enough, she thought. Valenti would

have no problem getting through that door, with a couple of guards to back him up.

Isabel yearned to run for her life and Max's. But she forced herself to stand still. She kept her focus on the molecules, making them move faster and faster until the metal doors got so hot, they began to melt. Then she allowed the molecules to slow. The doors cooled, but now they were sealed together.

Michael would be able to open them, if and when he got there. But anyone else would need at least a blowtorch.

That's right, Isabel told herself. Now you're thinking. And that's how you're going to get out of here.

She leaned against the wall and pressed her hands against her face. She felt the skin and bone move under her fingers as she changed her appearance to match that of the guard she knocked out.

Then she calmly made her way to the parking garage, got in the rental car, and took the elevator up. A few minutes later she was speeding through the desert.

"Hang on a little longer, Max," she whispered. "I'm almost there."

"Max, you've got to hang on," Liz cried. "Michael, Isabel, and Ray are going to be back here with the crystals any second."

"Yeah, Max," Alex added, only the slight tremor in his voice signaling what a wreck he actually was. "You can't check out now. You owe me a new car. One with air bags. Those babies are the only reason Maria and I are here talking to you."

Max opened his lips, but the only sound that came out was a wet clicking.

Is that what people call a death rattle? Liz thought wildly. No, he was still breathing. Shallow, ragged breaths that were painful to watch. And to hear.

"Should we help him sit up?" Maria asked. "Do you think that would help him breathe?"

Liz didn't know what to do. Should they be calling an ambulance? The paramedics could at least give him oxygen or something. But they'd take him to the hospital, and then if Michael, Isabel, and Ray showed up with the crystals, Max wouldn't be here.

And Max would die without the crystals, in the hospital or out of it.

"Liz," Max croaked out.

"I'm here," she told him. "Don't try to talk. Save your strength."

"Love . . . you." His eyelids fluttered shut.

"No!" Liz shouted. She grabbed him by the shoulders and shook him. His head flopped back and forth. "No, Max. Please, no."

"Is he?" Maria exclaimed, backing away from the bed.

"Check his pulse," Alex ordered. "Maybe he's just unconscious."

He was right. She didn't know for sure. She didn't hear the horrible, ragged breaths, but maybe. Maybe.

She pressed her fingers against the side of his neck. But her hands were shaking, and her own heartbeat was pounding in her ears. She couldn't tell.

"Max. Come on. I'm not letting you leave me,"

169

she cried. She reached out and gently slid up one of his eyelids. She thought she saw his pupil contract a little.

"I don't think . . . I think he's still with us," Liz exclaimed.

"Max, don't go into the light," Alex yelled.

Joking as usual. But Liz could hear the raw emotion in his voice.

"Max, we need you," Maria called. "You can't go yet."

Liz heard the squeal of tires outside the house. A second later the front door banged open.

"They're here! Did you hear that? They're back!" She checked his pupils again. This time there was no response. Liz felt as if her body had turned to seawater, heavy and cold.

"I've got them!" Isabel shouted as she exploded into the room.

"I . . . think it might be too late," Liz answered. She pressed her hand to Max's chest. She couldn't feel his heart beating.

"Try it, anyway," Alex demanded.

Isabel pulled the crystals out of her pockets and placed them in her brother's hand. She curled his fingers tight around them, keeping them closed with her own.

"You've got to connect to the consciousness, Max," Isabel told him.

"Please, Max," Liz begged. "You can't die on me now that you finally agreed we don't have to be just friends anymore."

170

Without realizing it, the entire crew had hud-
dled together at Max's bedside to support him.
Maria felt Isabel's hand on her shoulder and looked
up. Isabel's face was drained.

"Don't worry, Izzy. Max is gonna make it," Maria
whispered. "You brought the crystals . . . and now
he's gonna be all right."

Isabel looked straight at Maria, her eyes wide,
and exhaled.

"I hope you're right. Because Valenti's got Michael,"
she said.